GIRL LEAST LIKE TO MARRY

———

"Are you okay?"

Cassie nodded automatically, but she doubted she'd ever be okay again. She felt like she'd just had a lobotomy. Could a kiss render you stupid?

"I think I should go now. Unless..." He dropped his gaze to her swollen mouth.

Cassie shook her head and took a step back. *No unless.* Go, yes, just go. He'd turned her into a dunce.

Tuck smiled at her dazed look. It was nice to have left an impression on Little-Miss-Know-It-All. "Good night, Cassiopeia."

Cassie was incapable of answering him. She feared she'd been struck mute. As well as dumb. She watched him swagger to his room opposite hers, slot his key in, open his door. He turned as he stepped into his room.

"I'll be right over here. If you need a cup of *shhu-gar.*"

Cassie had no pithy comeback as his door clicked quietly shut.

DEAR READER,

I'm so excited to be involved in my very first Harlequin KISS continuity and to have worked with three authors who are not only wonderful writers but absolutely fabulous women! Writing a set of linked stories especially when each writer is separated by vast amounts of land and/or ocean can be challenging, but I think I can speak for all of us when I say we had a lot of fun during our online brainstorming sessions. I know for me there was something beautifully symbiotic about the depth of friendship between our four fictional friends and the way our friendships deepened over the course of the continuity.

I had a great time writing *Girl Least Likely to Marry,* affectionately known to us and those who follow me on Twitter as the #jock and the #geekgirl. I was very excited to be writing Cassiopeia, a bona fide Mensa-level genius. *Big Bang Theory* is one of my favourite TV shows and I really wanted to write a female Sheldon—although, not quite that extreme! But, I have to tell you, it was much more difficult than I ever imagined. As someone used to writing heroines with emotional depth, Cassie was a true challenge because while she had IQ to burn, her EQ was practically nonexistent. It took me quite a while to get a handle on her and I think I only really managed it by getting inside the hero's head. Tuck, in his laid-back Texan way, totally got Cassie. And getting to know him gave me a way to understand her.

I think out of all my heroes, I love Tuck the most. And that's not just because he's the kind of guy that belongs on a billboard advertising underwear (you know the kind, right?) but because his utterly alpha competitive spirit refused to let Cassie settle for the half-life she'd accepted as her lot.

I really hope you enjoy Cassie and Tuck's story about two people who weren't looking for love but found it anyway!

Love, Amy

GIRL
LEAST LIKELY
TO MARRY

———

AMY ANDREWS

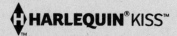

Recycling programs
for this product may
not exist in your area.

ISBN-13: 978-0-373-20724-4

GIRL LEAST LIKELY TO MARRY

Copyright © 2013 by Amy Andrews

HARLEQUIN®
www.Harlequin.com

ABOUT AMY ANDREWS

———

Amy Andrews has always loved writing, and still can't quite believe that she gets to do it for a living. Creating wonderful heroines and gorgeous heroes and telling their stories is an amazing way to pass the day. Sometimes they don't always act as she'd like them to—but then neither do her kids, so she's kind of used to it. Amy lives in the very beautiful Samford Valley, with her husband and aforementioned children, along with six brown chickens and two black dogs.

She loves to hear from her readers. Drop her a line at www.amyandrews.com.au.

Other Harlequin® KISS™ titles by Amy Andrews:

Driving Her Crazy

This and other titles by Amy Andrews are available in ebook format—check out **www.Harlequin.com**.

To Aimee Carson, Heidi Rice and Kimberly Lang.
Thanks for the laughs, ladies—
it was an absolute pleasure. Lets do it again sometime!

PS. A quick thank you to Aimee and Kim
who explained to me the meaning and context of
that great American word *jonesing*. I am a total convert
and plan on using it much, much more :-)

GIRL
LEAST LIKELY
TO MARRY

PROLOGUE

———

Ten years ago, Hillbrook University campus,
upstate New York…

CASSIOPEIA BARCLAY TAPPED the rim of her wine glass to the other three. 'Of course it's not the end,' she said, looking around at her fellow flatmates. 'Of course it's just the beginning. Tonight may be our last night together but not for long. We've got the road trip coming up soon, remember?'

The women all nodded in agreement although trust fund princess Reese looked quickly away, throwing back a hefty slug of her champagne. Gina, the Brit, followed suit, knocking her drink back with practised gusto. Southern Belle Marnie sipped regally, her good manners always on display.

Denying her Australian roots, Cassie also sipped her drink. Not because of good manners, or in deference to the expensive Dom Perignon that Reese and her Park Avenue pay cheque gave them access to—Cassie couldn't care less if she was drinking Dom or Dr Pepper—but because everything she did was calm and measured and logical.

Why down champagne, posh or otherwise, when it only led to a hangover?

Her first ever hangover had been here in this house, with these three women, and she had no desire to repeat the experience. That was the ultimate definition of stupidity.

And Cassiopeia Barclay was far from stupid.

In fact with an IQ of one hundred and sixty-three she was officially a genius.

Their attention was returned to the nearby athletic field, in plain view of their deckchairs. The sky was starting its slow slide into evening but Hillbrook's male track team could still easily be made out as they went through a training drill. It was a regular ritual for the 'Awesome Foursome', as they'd been dubbed, and Cassie joined in because these three women had been her family, accepting her social inadequacies without question, and they enjoyed it.

But, try as she might, she didn't get the fascination with either sport or the men who played it. Most of them were no doubt here on some trumped-up scholarship and Cassie found that pretty annoying. Why was it that there was no money to support scientific research but somehow there was always cash for another track field?

Gina sighed as a particularly buff guy leaned over, touching his toes, exposing the backs of his legs, his shorts riding up to reveal a peek at one taut buttock. 'Now, *that* is a well put together arse,' she murmured, her British accent even more pronounced in this very American setting.

Marnie rolled her eyes. The blonde from the Deep South was as different from the Englishwoman as was possible. She was petite and perky, with an innocence about her that stuck out like a sore thumb next to Gina's brash sexuality. But Cassie had seen Marnie come out of her shell over the course of the year, much like her, and a lot of that was owed to Gina and Reese's differing but vibrant influences.

Reese smiled at Gina indulgently. She'd been doing that a lot this last week, Cassie realised belatedly. Smiling. Gina's assertion earlier that it had something to do with a certain Marine had been confirmed by Reese's startling confession that said Marine was *the one.*

Imagine that! After a week!

Sometimes Cassie felt like an alien in their midst, and it was nothing to do with her Australian accent. Even at nineteen they all seemed sophisticated women of the world next to her, introverted geek girl—Marnie included.

Reese had just dropped the bombshell that she'd fallen in love at first sight, Gina was slowly working her way through the entire eligible—and not so eligible—male population of the United States, and Marnie was sighing over her friend's big white virginal wedding.

It was utterly perplexing, but also interesting—from a behavioural science perspective. How much more could her friends achieve if they locked up their hormones and concentrated on their chosen careers like she had? Still, these three women had opened her up to a whole world that she hadn't been aware of before, and all new experiences were beneficial.

Back home in Australia she'd led a largely solitary existence. Either at home with her parents, shut in her room and absorbed in some research or other, or at university doing the same thing.

There'd been no girlfriends. *No boyfriends.* No late-night drinking or ogling track teams.

But here at Hillbrook her 'gal pals'—yes, according to Gina they *were* gal pals—hadn't taken her social awkwardness, lack of fashion sense or inept dancing as an excuse. They'd dragged her to nightclubs and frat parties, and to bars where they served cocktails by the jug and Karaoke was King. They'd loaned her dresses and shoes, done her make-up and styled her hair and, most importantly, they hadn't taken no for an answer.

She had a lot to thank them for. She would look back on her year in the US as a social experiment, with her as the subject, from which she had collected some very useful data.

'One day, Gina,' Reese said, interrupting Cassie's train of thought, 'you are going to fall hard and fast for some guy, and I hope I'm going to be there to tell you I told you so!'

Marnie raised her glass. 'Cheers to that,' she said.

Gina scoffed in her very English way with a toss of her glossy dark hair. 'To hell with that.'

The others laughed as they returned to their regularly scheduled programming—the track team. Cassie followed suit, smiling at Gina's running commentary but perplexed by it at the same time. She was deeply thankful that jocks did nothing for her and that she was far too rational to be swayed by hormones.

Sure, as a scientist she understood that human beings were under the influence of their biological imperative to mate, but she also believed in head over heart. Certainly Gina wouldn't be in the quandary she was now if she'd been thinking with her brain instead of her ovaries.

Sleeping with Marnie's brother Carter last week had really rattled Gina. Cassie was generally fairly oblivious to nuances, but she'd have had to be deaf, dumb and blind to miss Gina's edginess. Quite why Gina was edgy Cassie had no idea. What was done was done. And it wasn't Gina who was engaged to be married, was it?

Which was exactly what she'd told Gina when she'd confessed the transgression to her last week and Gina had sworn her to secrecy.

It was at times like this that Cassie was glad she'd vowed never to fall victim to love. How could she when she simply didn't believe in it? And, even if she did, she didn't have time for the messy, illogical minefield of it all. Not while there was a big universe to study which was infinitely more fascinating than any man.

A shout of triumph from the track brought Cassie back into the conversation flowing around her.

'Mmm, that's right, my lovely blond Adonis.' Gina's commentary continued. 'Give your mate a hug, then.' The men complied, as if Gina had yanked their strings. 'Ding-dong,' she cooed on a happy sigh, and Marnie and Reese laughed.

Cassie watched the display of male camaraderie, rolling her eyes as they high-fived and man-hugged. They reminded her of gorillas. Next they'd be beating their chests and picking nits off each other. One thing was for sure: should she ever drop a hundred IQ points and end up with some man he would never be of the jock variety.

'Tell us about the stars, Cassie.'

Cassie glanced over at Marnie, whose head was dropped over the back of her chair as she pointed to the first star just visible in the sky. 'That's Venus, right... evening star?'

Cassie smiled. Marnie was forever talking about the night skies over Savannah and had loved having her own personal astronomer at her beck and call. 'Yep,' she confirmed, looking at the pinprick of light in the velvet sky.

'Will we be able to see Cassiopeia tonight?' she asked.

Cassie shook her head. 'It's too light here. When we're on our road trip we'll stop at the Barringer Crater in Arizona. We'll sleep under the stars and I'll show you then.'

It was the main reason Cassie was going on the trip. Time with her gal pals would be great, but she'd always wanted to see the crater site formed when a meteorite had ploughed into the earth fifty thousand years ago, and that was her priority.

'You speak for yourself,' Gina butted in. 'The only stars the Park Avenue Princess and I are sleeping under are of the five-star variety. Isn't that right, Reese?'

Reese nodded. 'Er...yes,' she said, looking quickly away and taking another decent slug of her champers.

'Carter proposed to Missy under the stars at the Grand Canyon. Isn't that romantic?' she said, her voice dreamy. 'Our families were on holiday together. Missy and I stayed up all night talking about how wonderful it was.'

'Bless their hearts,' Gina said, mimicking Marnie's Southern drawl.

It had taken Cassie a few months of Gina teasing Marnie over the quaint Southern phrase to realise it could be used to mock as well as to sweeten. Glancing at Gina's tense profile, she guessed this was one of the mocking times.

'Missy wants a star theme running through the reception,' Marnie continued ignoring Gina's sarcasm. 'She's spending a small fortune on this gorgeous black drapery that billows from the ceiling and twinkles with thousands of tiny lights...'

Cassie didn't really understand why you'd spend good money on creating the illusion of a starry sky when the real thing was up there for free. It certainly didn't seem to be very effective budgeting. But weddings were as much a mystery to her as the notion of love, so she gave up trying to figure it out.

She was just going to lounge here with her friends and watch the stars come out.

One last time.

ONE

A decade on…

    CASSIOPEIA WATCHED TUCK… whatever his last name was…of quarterback fame swagger in the general direction of their table with his long, loose-limbed gait. Somehow his big, blond athleticism seemed to dominate the vast expanse of the open tent, with its delicate swathes of royal blue draped across the ceilings and trailing gently to the deck. But then she had a feeling he'd probably dominate any setting.

He made slow progress. Men stopped him to slap him on the back and shake his hand. Women stopped him to bat their eyelashes and put their hands on him. He took both in his stride, shrugging off their adoration with a wide, easy *Shucks, I ain't nuthin'* grin. The man was so laid-back Cassie was surprised he managed to stay vertical.

Very different from the man she'd watched only yesterday playing a very physical game of one-on-one basketball with Reese's ex-Marine ex-husband Mason.

Reese had left the party that had originally been intended to be her wedding to Dylan to go after Mason, but her instructions to the remaining members of the Awesome Foursome had been clear—make sure no one gets into a fight.

Reese had deliberately sat Tuck, the jilted groom's best man, next to her—away from Gina—to prevent such a calamity.

With Tuck firmly on Team Dylan and Gina, whose favourite pastime was baiting people, on Team Reese, Cassie could already tell it was going to be a long night.

'He sure is pretty,' Gina murmured with relish as she tracked his progress.

A very long night.

Cassie didn't really see the attraction. But then she'd never been a slave to her hormones. She just wasn't programmed that way.

Sure, Tuck Whats-his-name had all the features that the female of the species looked for in a mate. He was tall, broad-shouldered, narrow-hipped. She couldn't see the delineation of the muscles in his chest tonight, although they were obviously there beneath his charcoal suit. She knew from his shirtless one-on-one yesterday that they were plentiful and very well developed.

And, in the animal world, muscles equalled strength. Another biological tick in his favour.

There was also the symmetry of his face. Square jaw, prominent cheekbones, nose, chin and forehead all proportional. Eyes evenly spaced. Lips perfectly aligned. Facial symmetry was one of the big markers of physical attraction and worthiness for mating, and Tuck had it in spades.

But Cassie still didn't get it.

'I have to go to the bathroom,' she said, turning to Gina. 'Try not to get into a fight with him while I'm gone. Remember, Reese is counting on us.'

'I'll be on my best behaviour,' Gina assured her.

If Cassie had been better at picking up sarcasm she wouldn't have been assured one iota, but she nodded, satisfied.

'Here—reapply,' Gina said, reaching into her clutch purse and pulling out the deep mulberry lipstick she'd slathered on Cassie's mouth earlier.

Cassie frowned. 'Why?'

'Because.' Gina sighed. 'That's the price of wearing lippy.' She waggled the item at her friend, who was looking at it as if it were a foreign object she'd never seen before. 'Beauty is pain.'

Cassie smiled at the old catchphrase. *Beauty is pain.* She'd learned many things about being a woman under Gina's tutelage. Gina could wear a pair of killer stilettos out clubbing all night without a single wince. Cassie had pretty much forgotten everything in the intervening decade, but she'd never forgotten how Gina had taken her under her wing—as if she were an Antipodean Eliza Doolittle.

Of course Cassie had failed 'Female 101' resoundingly, but Gina had been sweet and patient and there was just something about her vibrant personality that drew people. Cassie and Gina had stayed in contact despite the wedge that had been driven between the Awesome Foursome after Gina had thrown her one-night stand with Carter in Marnie's face that fateful last night together ten years ago.

And now, a decade down the track, Gina was still looking out for her in the fashion stakes. Gina had taken one look at the shapeless maxi-dress Cassie had been going to wear and declared it an unnatural disaster. Before Cassie had known it she was swathed in soft grape fabric with no sleeves, a plunging crossover neckline, a ruched form-fitting waist and an A-line skirt, the hem of which fluttered just below her knees.

Her straight brown hair had been freed from its regulation floral scrunchie and loosely curled. Sparkly, strappy kitten heels had been supplied. A subtle hand had seen to eyeshadow and mascara. Lipstick had been brandished with gusto.

'Reapply,' Gina repeated.

Bowing to a greater knowledge, Cassie took the lipstick as instructed and departed.

Tuck pulled up at the table he'd been allocated a minute later. His knee ached but he ignored it in deference to the sultry sex goddess with raven hair. She was dressed in something red and clingy, sitting there looking up at him with a smile on her full mouth. A connoisseur of women from way back, he liked what he saw.

He shot her one of his killer smiles. He knew they were killer because an article about him in *Cosmo* had spent an entire paragraph talking about the sheer wickedness of his smile.

'Well this here may just be my lucky night,' he drawled,

deliberately dragging out his vowels, plying her with all his Southern charm. His accent had been blunted over the years, with travel and living far from his Texan roots, but he could still pull it out when required.

According to the magazines, women just loved all that Southern country-boy charisma.

Gina quirked an elegantly arched eyebrow. 'Oh, yes? Do tell,' she murmured.

'Ah, you're the Brit.' He grinned. 'Gina, right?'

She nodded. 'And you're the quarterback.'

Tuck checked the closest handwritten place card on the table, disappointed to see that he was sitting directly opposite this sexy Englishwoman. He held it up and looked at her. 'What say we switch this one for whoever's supposed to be sitting next to you?'

'Hmm...' Gina placed her elbows on the table, propping her chin on one palm, pretending to think. 'I think Reese meant to keep you and I apart.'

Tuck shot her his best wounded look. 'And why would she want to do that?'

'I think she was afraid you and I might come to blows.'

He continued his *faux* outrage. 'Over what?'

'Over her recent...shall we say...split from the groom. *Your* best friend?'

'Ah. Well, now, if Dylan's unconcerned then there's no good in me holding a grudge, is there? Besides,' Tuck said, pulling out his chair and sitting, his knee protesting at the movement, 'I can flirt just as well from this side.'

Gina laughed. She couldn't help herself. The big

blond quarterback had an ego the size of North America. 'You're *that* good, huh?'

'Darlin', I am *the* best.'

Gina spied Cassie in the distance, making her way back to the table. She flicked her gaze to Tuck. It would be good to see him brought down a notch or two. 'Works every time, huh?'

Tuck grinned at the sudden sparkle of light he could see in her eyes. '*Every* time.'

'No one's immune to your charm?'

Tuck shook his head. 'Women love me. If they're female and breathing...' He shrugged, then dazzled her with another wide smile. 'What can I say? I have a gift.'

Gina smiled back. He really was an exceedingly good-looking man, and his cast-iron confidence only added to his allure. It was a shame she wasn't in the right frame of mind for a dalliance because she had an idea a night in bed with Tuck would be a great way to forget how badly she'd stuffed up all those years ago.

But her heart wasn't in it.

Just then the DJ played his first number for the night and Tuck pressed home the advantage. 'Ah, they're playing our song,' he teased. 'How about we knock off the pretence and you just dance with me, Gina?'

Gina considered him a moment, aware of Cassie drawing closer all the time behind Tuck's head. 'Nah, getting me to dance would be too easy. Care to take a little wager?'

Tuck smiled at her. A woman who liked to gamble—better and better. He leaned forward. 'I'm all ears.'

'I bet you can't get her—' Gina nodded her head to indicate Cassie '—to dance.'

Tuck turned in his chair to see who Gina had in mind for him. A woman about the same age as Gina in some kind of purple dress was walking towards them. She had long dark brown hair arranged in loose ringlets that fell forward over nice bare shoulders. She had a cute nose, pretty eyes and an interesting mouth, and she was walking along seemingly oblivious to her surroundings, a slight frown marring her forehead as if her thoughts were somewhere else.

She was no English sex kitten, that was for sure.

She didn't look like the average gridiron groupie either. Still, she was female, and Tuck had always liked a challenge. He turned back and smiled at Gina. 'Piece of cake.'

Gina laughed. 'Oh, this is going to be good.'

Tuck raised an eyebrow. 'What do I get? When I win?'

Gina smiled. 'The pleasure of Cassie's company, of course.'

Tuck inclined his head. 'Of course.'

Despite her earlier concerns about leaving Gina and Tuck together, Cassie had given it little thought in the fifteen minutes she'd been away. Her brain had been mulling over the findings of an astronomy research paper she'd read last night. She'd even applied the lipstick as ordered by Gina without conscious thought as she recalled the fascinating data.

She was surprised for a moment when she arrived back at the table to find Tuck Whats-his-name sitting there with Gina, apparently getting along just fine. She slotted the research into a file in her head and shut it down with a mental mouse click.

'Everything okay here?' she asked.

Tuck took a deep breath, then stood and used one of his very best *hey-baby* smiles on Cassie. 'Hi,' he said. 'I'm Reese's cousin, Tuck.' He stuck out his hand. 'It's mighty fine to meet you, ma'am.'

Cassie blinked up at him as he towered over her. Two things struck her at once. The man smelled incredible. Her nostrils flared as her senses filled up with him. And it wasn't his cologne, because she was pretty sure she couldn't smell anything artificial at all. Maybe a hint of soap or deodorant.

This was much rawer. More primal. Powerful. Over-powering, even. It made her want to press her nose to his shirt and inhale him. It *demanded* that she do so and she had to actually put her hands on the chair-back to stop herself.

So this was pheromones.

Scientists had known of their existence for decades, and perfume companies around the world had been try-ing to perfect them for just as long, but this man exuded it in hot, sticky waves.

Her salivary glands went into hyper-drive and she swallowed as she grappled with the urge to sniff him.

The second thing was his eyes. They were an intense, startling blue. The exact shade of an exploding star she'd once seen through the lens of a deep space telescope. They were out of this world. They were cosmic. Capti-vating.

Tuck looked into Cassie's upturned face. She was staring at him, her lips slightly parted, the sound of her breath husky in his ears. He glanced at Gina and grinned.

Piece of cake.

'Ma'am?'

Cassie dragged herself back from the universe she could see in his eyes, his intoxicating scent still singing to her like a Siren from the rocks. 'Oh, yes...sorry.' She shook her head. What had he said? Name. He'd introduced himself. 'I'm Cassie,' she said. 'Cassiopeia.'

And then she made the mistake of slipping her hand into his and his pheromones tugged at her—hard.

'So you're the geek,' he said softly, smiling at her.

Another dizzying wave of male animal wafted over her and it took a moment for Cassie's brain to clear the fog.

Yes, she was the geek. And he was the jock. She had him by a good sixty IQ points—probably more. She didn't get stupid around men. She didn't get stupid, period!

So start acting like it!

She pulled her hand from his abruptly. 'And you're the *jock*,' she said, as much to remind herself as a statement of fact.

Tuck refused to be offended. He shot Gina a *faux* insulted look. 'Why do I get the feeling that Cassie isn't fond of jocks?'

Gina lifted a shoulder. 'Don't take it personally. Cassie's not fond of men generally.' He shot her a look and she cut him off before he gave voice to what she knew he was thinking. 'Not women, either.'

Tuck grinned, then turned his attention back to Cassie. Okay, so he had his work cut out for him. His momma always said things came too damn easy to him anyway. Her eyes were even prettier up close. A grey-blue, like a misty lake, with subtle charcoal and silver eyeshadow bringing out both colours perfectly.

He nodded at her place card on the table next to his and said, 'Looks like I have the whole night to change your mind.' Then he pulled out her chair and smiled at her.

Cassie didn't move for a moment. She simply stared at him as the deep modulation of his voice joined forces with his heady scent to drench every cell in her body with a sexual malaise. Her nipples beading against the fabric of the flimsy dress Gina had loaned her snapped her out of it.

'I usually require several pieces of evidence from trusted sources before I change my mind about anything,' she said primly, taking the seat.

'Noted,' Tuck murmured, stifling a grin as he took his seat. He lounged back in it, regarding Cassie as she fiddled with her cutlery. 'So, you don't sound like you're from around these here parts,' he said.

'No.' Cassie refused to elaborate. Just because Reese thought it was a good idea to sit them together, it didn't mean she had to be agreeable.

Gina rolled her eyes and took pity on Tuck. 'Cassie's Australian.'

'Ah. Whereabouts? Sydney? That's one pretty little city you have there,' he said.

'Canberra,' Cassie said as she ran her finger up and

down the flat of her knife. 'It's the capital,' she added. A lot of people didn't realise that.

And he *was* a jock.

'Well, now,' he said, leaning forward in his chair, his gaze acknowledging Gina before returning to Cassie, 'we can have us a meeting of the United Nations.'

'Hardly,' Cassie said, desperately trying to sit as far back in her chair as possible and remember that he was a jock—a *footballer*—even if he did have pheromones so potent he should be being studied at the Smithsonian. Or milked and sold to the highest-bidding perfume manufacturer.

'There are one hundred and ninety-three member states in the United Nations. And they meet in Geneva.' She looked at Tuck. Jocks weren't very good with geography. 'That's in Switzerland.'

Tuck raised an eyebrow. He was used to people making assumptions about his intelligence. Truth be told, he played up to them mostly—because calling people on their ignorance was usually an amusing way to pass the time.

It looked as if he was going to have a whole lot of fun with Cassie. 'That's just north of Ireland, right?'

Cassie pursed her lips. 'It's in Europe.'

'Europe? *Dang,*' Tuck said, broadening his accent. 'I'm always getting them muddled up.'

'Of course if you're talking about the Security Council,' Cassie plunged on, as the deep twang in his accent twanged some invisible strings low down inside her she'd never known existed, 'that's in New York. And you'd be in luck as Australia has just scored a seat on the Security Council.'

Tuck shot a look at Gina, who winked and grinned, clearly enjoying herself. Tuck was about to say something like, *They wear those funny blue helmets at the Security Council, right?* But the imperious tones of his and Reese's Great-Aunt Ada interrupted.

'Samuel Tucker,' she said in her brash, booming New York accent. 'How'd you sneak in here undetected?'

Tuck stood and smiled down at the self-appointed matriarch of the family. A died-in-the-wool Yankee, she liked to pretend that the Southern branch didn't exist most of the time, but he had a soft spot for the sharp-tongued octogenarian.

'Aunt Ada,' he said, sweeping her up in his arms for a hearty hug. 'Still as pretty as a picture, I see.'

Cassie felt herself sag a little as Tuck and his overwhelming masculinity gave her some breathing space.

'Don't sweet-talk me, young man. What are you doing all the way over here?'

Tuck gestured to the table. 'I'm keeping Reese's friends company.'

'Reese...' Ada tutted. 'Running off after that Marine... That girl hasn't got the sense she was born with...lucky she's my favourite.'

'Now, come on, Aunt Ada,' Tuck teased. 'I thought *I* was your favourite.' Ada gave him a playful pat on the shoulder, then lifted one gnarled old hand and squeezed his cheek.

Gina's mobile rang and she almost ignored it. She couldn't decide what was more fascinating—the big blond quarterback sweet-talking an old lady or Cassie's deer-in-the-headlights face. But it rang insistently, and Ada turned to her, looking imperiously down her nose.

'Well, girl, are you going to answer that or not?'

Gina, recognising authority when she saw it, picked it up immediately. The screen display flashed a familiar number. 'It's Reese,' she announced.

'Reese.' Ada tutted again. 'Tell her to get back here. This non-wedding party was *her* hare-brained idea.'

Gina laughed, but as she answered the phone Ada's interest had already wandered.

Cassie felt her shrewd gaze next.

'This your girl?' she said, turning to Tuck.

'Absolutely not,' Cassie said indignantly.

Then Tuck undid his jacket button and it fell open, wafting a heady dose of pheromones her way. She shut her eyes briefly as her pulse spiked in primal response.

'She's not your usual type,' Ada said, ignoring Cassie's denial.

'I am *not* his girl,' Cassie repeated, even though she could practically hear every cell calling his name.

'It's okay,' Ada assured her. 'I hate his usual type. Too...fussy.'

Tuck looked down at Cassie. She was frowning at him, her eyebrows weren't plucked, and she wasn't wearing a single scrap of jewellery. No one in the world would have described her as fussy. And yet there was something rather intriguing about her...

'We are *not* together,' Cassie reiterated. The thought was utterly preposterous.

'Reese says she and Mason aren't coming back tonight,' Gina announced as she terminated the phone call, interrupting the conversation.

'Right, then,' Ada said. 'Looks like we have a show to be getting on with. Samuel, go and tell that dreadful DJ to announce dinner. I'll get the wait staff to start serving.'

The three of them watched her sweep away. 'Wow,' Gina said. 'She's scary.'

Tuck grinned. 'Hell, yeah. Excuse me, Gina, Cassio-peia.' He dropped his voice an octave, then bowed at her slightly, finding and holding her gaze. 'Keep my seat warm, darlin', I won't be long.'

Cassie gaped as his cosmic blue eyes pierced her to the spot and his voice washed over her in tidal wave of heat.

Gina's low throaty laughter barely registered.

Two hours later Cassie was strung so tight every muscle was screaming at her. Tuck was holding court at the table, charming all and sundry.

Big, warm-blooded, male and there.

A giant sex gland, emitting a chemical compound her body was, *apparently,* biologically programmed to crave.

Him. A *jock.* Why *him?*

Every time their arms brushed or his thigh pressed briefly along hers her pulse spiked, her hands shook a little. And when he laughed in that whole body way of his, which he did frequently, throwing his head back, baring the heavy thud of his jugular to her gaze, her nostrils flared and filled with the thick, luscious scent of him.

An insistent voice whispered through her head, pounded through her blood. *Smell him. Lick him. Touch him*. With every tick of the clock, every beat of her heart, it grew louder.

It was insane. Madness.

This sort of thing didn't happen to her. Hormones. Primal imperatives. She was above bodily urges. Her head always—*always*—ruled her body.

But here she was, just like the rest of the human race, at the mercy of biology.

It just didn't compute.

The man was as dumb as a rock. He'd thought they were talking about food when she'd mentioned Pi. He'd called a truly amazing piece of equipment unlocking the secrets of the universe the *Hobble* telescope. He didn't even know the Vice-President of his own country.

He was a Neanderthal.

But still every nerve in her body twitched in a state of complete excitement.

Cassie desperately tried to recall the aurora research waiting in her room—the research she'd been looking forward to getting back to at the end of the night. When was the last time she'd gone two hours without thinking about it? She'd been working on the project for five years. She ate, slept, breathed it.

And for two whole hours it had been the *furthest* thing from her mind.

Marnie laughed at something Tuck said, dragging Cassie's attention back to the big blond caveman by her side. She checked her watch—was it too early to leave? She wasn't used to feeling this out of her depth. Sure, social situations weren't her forte but this was plain torture. If she could get back to her room and the comfort of the familiar Tuck and the awful persistent thrum in her blood would surely fade to black.

She glanced up at Gina, who shook her head and mouthed, 'Don't even think of it.'

Cassie sighed, resigned to her fate, as the raunchy strains of *Sweet Home Alabama* blasted around them. Marnie whooped and leapt up to dance along with a few others from the table.

Tuck looked across at Gina and winked. He stood and looked down at the woman who had sat beside him for two hours as if she was afraid his particular brand of stupid was contagious. Didn't she *know* he was God's gift to women?

He grinned as he held out his hand towards her. 'What do you say, Cassiopeia? Fancy a dance?'

Cassie stared at his hand. It was big, and she swore she could see waves of whatever the hell he was emitting undulating seductively from his palm. 'Oh, no.' She shook her head. 'I don't dance.'

Tuck hadn't got to where he was today by giving up at the first hurdle. He kept his hand where it was. 'It's not hard, darlin',' he murmured. 'Just hang on and follow my lead.'

Cassie swallowed. That was what she was afraid of. She had a very bad feeling she'd follow that intoxicating scent anywhere. She shook her head again and looked at him. A bad move as his cosmic gaze sucked her in closer to his orbit.

'I'm a terrible dancer,' she said. She dragged her gaze from him. 'Isn't that right, Gina?'

Gina nodded. Cassie had no rhythm at all. 'She speaks

the truth. But...' She looked at Tuck, then at Cassie. Her Antipodean friend looked as if she'd rather face a firing squad then dance with Tuck. *Interesting*. She'd never seen Cassie so ruffled and, bet or no bet, she wanted to see where this went.

'I think every woman should dance with a star quarterback once in her life,' Gina said.

Tuck raised an eyebrow at her as Gina conceded the bet to him.

'Ex,' Cassie said. And when Gina looked at her enquiringly she clarified, 'He's an ex...quarterback.'

Gina drummed her fingers on the table. 'You know, it *is* customary at weddings for the bridesmaids to dance with the groomsmen,' she pointed out.

Gina had taken it upon herself to be Cassie's social guru during the year they'd roomed together, and Cassie had learned a lot about social mores that no textbook could ever have taught her. But she was big on survival instincts, and Cassie was pretty sure staying away from Tuck was the smart thing to do.

And she was very smart.

Even if she was rapidly dropping IQ points every time she looked at him.

'But this is the wedding-that-wasn't,' she pointed out, striving for the brisk logic she was known for. 'We are the bridal-party-that-wasn't. Surely that cancels out societal expectations?'

Tuck waggled the fingers of his still outstretched hand at her. 'I think it's important to keep up appearances, though,' he said. 'These Park Avenue types are big on that.'

Cassie looked away from the lure of those fingers at Gina, who nodded at her and said, 'He's right. You wouldn't want to embarrass Reese, would you? It's okay,' she assured her. 'Tuck looks like he knows what he's doing.'

Tuck grinned, but he didn't take his eyes off Cassie. 'Yes, ma'am.'

Cassie glanced back at him, towering over her in all his intoxicating temptation. Maybe a dance would help. Maybe if she got the chance to sniff him a little this unnatural craving taking over her body, infecting her brain like a plague of boils, would be satisfied. That seemed logical.

Cassie slipped her hand into his.

And her cells roared to life.

TWO

———

BY THE TIME they got to the dance floor the last notes of *Sweet Home Alabama* had died out and the music had changed to a slow Righteous Brothers' melody. All the couples that had been boogying energetically melted into each other and the singles left the floor. Cassie turned to go as well, but Tuck grabbed her hand and pulled her in close, grinning at her.

'Where are you going, darlin'?'

Cassie's breath felt like thick fog in her throat. 'I... can't waltz.'

She found it hard enough co-ordinating her hands and feet with some space between her and her dancing partners. She was going to do some damage to his feet for sure.

And she did not trust herself too close to him.

'Sure you can. Just hold on,' he said, taking her resisting hands and placing them on his pecs, 'and shuffle your feet a little. There ain't no dance police here tonight.'

Cassie didn't hear his crack about dance police. Her

palms were filled with hard firm muscle as the fabric seemed to melt away. The music melted away too—as did the people crowding around them.

She couldn't take her eyes off the sight of her hands on his chest.

Tuck smiled to himself. 'There you go—see.' He took a step closer, his chin brushing the top of her head. He slipped his hands lightly onto her waist. There was definite curve there and he snuggled his palm into it. 'I don't bite.'

Cassie fought through the fog, dragging her eyes away from how small her hands looked in comparison to his broadness. She looked up. Way up. He was tall. And close. A hand-width away, she guessed.

Before tonight she would have been able to assess the distance accurately, but she simply couldn't think straight at the moment. He was radiating heat and energy and those damn pheromones, totally scrambling her usual focus. His hands at her waist were burning a tract right down to her middle.

He smiled at her, his starburst eyes showering their effervescence all over her. She looked down, but that was a mistake also as his chest filled her vision, the knot of his tie swaying hypnotically in front of her with every movement of his body. And all the time an insistent whisper played in her head, swarmed through her blood in time with the swing of him.

Smell him, lick him, touch him.

She dragged her gaze upwards, desperate to stop the pull of the hypnotic rhythm. It snagged on the slow, steady bound of his carotid, his growth of whiskers not able to conceal the thick thud of it. She wondered what he'd smell like there. What he'd taste like.

Her nostrils flared. Her breath grew thick. She dug her fingers into the flat of his chest as she battled the urge to take a step closer.

Dear God, she was growing dumber by the second.

Shocked and dazed, she dragged her gaze down. Way down. Down to their feet. Down to the hole she wished would open up.

Tuck also looked down, frowning at how rigid she felt in his arms. As if she was going to shatter at any moment. Or going to bolt at any second. No woman had ever been so reluctant to be in his company. Or so keen to be away from it.

She could give a man a complex.

One thing was for sure. She needed to relax or she was going to have a seizure. 'So...Cassiopeia? That's not a name you hear every day. Is that a family tradition?'

Cassie looked up. His eyes flashed at her and she lost her breath for a moment. Were they closer? He seemed nearer. More potent. His chest was closer.

'Cassie?'

She blinked. What? Oh, yes. Talking. That was good. She was good at talking. Usually...

'My mum...she named me. After the constellation.' She paused. Did he even know what that was? 'That's a group of stars,' she clarified.

Tuck chuckled. This woman was going to give him a complex. Who'd have thought he'd be interested in such a little snob? The endearing thing was she seemed oblivious to it all. 'Like the Zodiac?' he enquired, purposefully broadening his accent again.

Cassie gaped at him. How could she possibly want to lick the neck of a man with a pea-sized intellect?

There was just no accounting for biology.

'No, *not* like the Zodiac.'

He feigned a frown. 'Ain't you into astrology?'

'Astronomy,' she said, gritting her teeth. '*A-stron-omy.*'

'So, that's not like...Sagittarius and stuff?'

'No,' she said primly. 'It's the study of celestial objects. It's *science.* Not voodoo.'

Tuck laughed again. He liked it when she got all passionate and fired up. There was a spark in those blue-grey eyes, a glitter. Would they get like that when she was all passionate and fired up in bed?

Suddenly it seemed like something he wouldn't mind knowing.

The song ended and the pace picked up a little. A couple behind them bumped into Cassie and she stumbled and stood on his foot. 'Oh, God, sorry,' she gasped, pulling away as her front collided with his.

His broad, muscular front.

'Hey, there, it's okay,' Tuck said, steadying her under her elbows, holding on as she tried to pull away, keeping her close. Their bodies were almost—but not quite—touching. 'No harm done,' he said, smiling at her. 'Why don't you just lay your head here on my chest and stay awhile longer?'

She should tell him to go to hell. But her nostrils flared again as something primal inside her recognised him as male. And he smelled so damn good.

A whisper ran through her head. *Do it.*

Lay your head down. Shut your eyes. Press your nose into his chest.

Cassie fought against the powerful urge as long as she could but she was losing fast. Each sway of his body bathed her in his *eau-du*-male scent and before she knew it her cheek had brushed against the fabric of his jacket and was angled slightly, her nose pressed into his lapel.

She inhaled. Deep and long. Every cell was filled with him. Every tastebud went into rapture. Every brain synapse went into a frenzy.

It was so damn good she never wanted to exhale.

It was only the dizzying approach of hypoxia that forced her hand. She quickly breathed out, then took in another huge greedy gulp of him. His scent seduced her senses, stroked along her belly, unfurled through her bloodstream.

She pressed herself a little closer and her eyes rolled back in her head as his heat flooded all round her.

Tuck was surprised when Cassie's body moved flush against his after her standoffishness. But he liked the way she fitted, her body moulding against his, her head tucked in under his chin nicely. And she let him lead, which was a novelty. Most women he danced with weren't so passive in his arms.

They danced all flirty and dirty and sexy.

Not that Tuck had anything against *flirty, dirty* or *sexy*. He was all for them. But too often it felt like an act. As if the women he dated felt they *had* to gyrate and shimmy and generally carry on like a B-grade porn star to attract or keep his attention.

Okay, he'd never had a reputation for longevity—his two-year marriage was a sure sign of that—but he was, at his most basic, a guy. And just being *female* was enough to keep his attention.

Ever since his divorce he'd gone back to his partying ways—living the dream, a different woman every night—the ultimate male fantasy. But he'd forgotten how good this felt, how nice it was to slow-dance, to hold a woman and enjoy the feeling of her all relaxed against him.

Even if she did think he was dumb as a rock.

'I think you've got this dancing thing down pat, darlin',' he murmured against her hair.

Cassie just heard him through the trancelike state she'd entered. Each breath she drew in fogged her head a little more, stroking along nerve-endings and leadening her bones. She was pretty sure she was drooling on his jacket.

But he had her in his thrall.

His hands felt big and male on her hips, and hot—very hot. She was aware of every part of her body. It was alive with the scent of him.

His chin rubbed the top of her head and she glanced up. Her gaze fell on the heavy thud of his carotid again, pulsing just above his collar beside the hard ridge of his trachea. Her mouth watered a little more and Cassie sucked in a breath.

'Well, *hey,* y'all!'

Cassie dragged herself back from the impulse to push her nose into Tuck's neck, grateful for Marnie's interruption. She looked at her friend, who was dancing with a preppy-looking guy, still a little dazed.

'It's getting hot in here,' Marnie said, then winked as her partner danced her away.

Cassie blinked at her retreating back and then glanced at Tuck, who was looking intently at her with his intense extra-terrestrial gaze.

What was she thinking?

She searched her brain for an answer. How great he smelled. How great he might taste. But more than that. She'd been thinking how small and feminine she felt tucked in under his chin, his hands shaping her hips.

How female.

She blinked, shocked by her thoughts. Since when had she cared about that? But her gaze was filled with his perfect symmetrical features and it all became fuzzy again. Why couldn't he have a prominent forehead and squinty eyes and a crooked nose? He was a footballer, for crying out loud, didn't they break noses regularly?

Why didn't she feel like this about Len, her fellow researcher-cum-occasional-lover? She'd never once had to quell the urge to sniff *him*. They worked together every day, occasionally accompanied each other to university functions, and every once in a while he got antsy and irritable and they had sex, so he could concentrate on what was really important—astronomy.

She'd never slow-danced with Len. Nor did she want to.

She'd never wanted to crawl inside his skin.

It was a scary thought, and Cassie tried to pull away as another slow song started up, but Tuck held her fast and her damn body capitulated readily. Too readily. It was obvious biology was going to win out over intellect and logic tonight and that just wasn't acceptable.

She needed to defuse the situation, to distract herself from the dizzying power of him.

'So,' she said, reaching for a safe, easy topic of conversation, 'Tuck isn't your real name?'

It was hardly Mensa level, and they weren't about to unlock the secrets of dark matter, but at least it would give her back some control.

Mind over body.

And he looked like a guy who liked to talk about himself.

'No.' Tuck shook his head. 'My Christian name is Samuel. Samuel Tucker. But no one calls me that. Except my mother.'

Even his wife had called him Tuck.

'And Great-Aunt Ada,' Cassie reminded him.

Tuck smiled. 'And Great-Aunt Ada.'

Cassie frowned. 'Why not be called by the name you were given?'

Tuck shrugged. 'It's a nickname.' He looked down into her genuinely perplexed face. 'Don't they have nicknames in Australia? You're called Cassie instead of Cassiopeia.'

Cassie shook her head. 'No. Cassie is an *abbreviation* of my Christian name, not a nickname. If that were the case for you, you'd be known as Sam.'

Tuck waited for her to spell *abbreviation* for his poor addled brain. If she hadn't felt a hundred kinds of right, all smooshed up and slow dancing against him, he'd be getting kind of ticked off by her attitude towards his mental prowess.

Instead he was prepared to humour her.

'Except Tuck sounds cooler.'

Cassie frowned. '*Cooler*? Who says?'

Tuck liked the way her brows drew together, showcasing her grey-blue eyes to perfection. 'Tens of thousands of football fans, screaming my name across every state in this great land for a decade.'

Not to mention quite a few more of the female variety also screaming it out loud in hotel beds across every state for just as long.

'Oh.' Cassie thought about it for a moment, but she'd never understood the dynamics of hero-worship regarding something as frivolous as sport. 'Sorry, I don't get that.'

He shrugged. 'It's a guy thing.'

Cassie suspected it was probably a *jock* thing, but she tucked it away anyway to ask Len about when they next spoke.

Thankfully the song ended and, feeling more in control of her recalcitrant hormones, she took the opportunity to step firmly away from him. 'I'm done now,' she said, and was proud of how strong her voice sounded when her body was howling to be nearer to him.

Tuck smiled and bowed slightly, ever the gentleman, as he gestured for her to precede him. It didn't stop him from perving on her ass the whole way back to the table, though.

Almost two hours later everyone had left and Marnie, Gina and Cassie, under the direction of Great-Aunt Ada, had seen all the guests off and organised the removal of the gifts that had been left despite Reese insisting that no one bring any.

Tuck and his pheromones had also insisted on helping.

Cassie was getting twitchy. She had a paper to get back to. She didn't have time for a big, blond ex-quarterback who'd obviously fallen out of the stupid tree. And hit every branch on the way down.

No matter how nice he smelled.

But somehow he was accompanying them back inside the grand entrance to the Bellington Estate, and then he was walking up the ornate stone staircase next to her, his arm occasionally brushing hers. When Marnie and Gina turned left at the top Cassie hoped that Tuck would do so too.

No such luck.

He smiled at her as he turned right. 'After you,' he said.

Cassie looked over her shoulder at Gina and Marnie, who had stopped and were looking at her with bemused expressions.

Gina waved her fingers and said, 'Need someone to *tuck* you in?'

Marnie seemed to have trouble keeping a straight face and Cassie frowned at her.

'I think she's got that covered,' Marnie said. 'Night, Cassie. Night, Tuck. Sweet dreams.'

Cassie glanced at Tuck, who was also smiling.

'Good night, ladies. See you in the morning.'

Before Cassie could make further comment her

'friends' had turned away and she was watching their backs retreat. She hoped that Marnie and Gina would use the time to talk, because it had been awkward between them at the table tonight. Although if the distance between them as they walked was anything to go by it didn't look like they were ready to bury the hatchet just yet.

She looked at Tuck, and even though he was a good two metres away his aroma wafted her way and she instantly forgot about the animosity between her friends. Her belly tightened and then looped the loop.

'What's your room number? I'll see you to your door.'

The last thing Cassie wanted was to have Tuck anywhere near her room. In fact she'd be perfectly happy never to be anywhere near him again. She was unsettled. Confused.

She was never unsettled. Never confused. And she didn't like it. Not one bit.

'I don't need you to accompany me to my room,' she said, taking care as she passed him to keep her distance.

Tuck watched the swing of her ass again for a moment or two, then called after her, 'My momma would tan my hide if I didn't see my date to her door.'

Cassie stopped mid-stride and turned to face him. 'I am *not* your date.'

'You sure danced like I was your date.'

Heat flooded her cheeks as she remembered how she'd clung and buried her nose in his clothes, as if he was her own personal scratch-and-sniff jock. Cassiopeia Barclay did *not* blush—ever! Curious at the strange phenomenon, she brought her palms up to cradle her face.

She cleared her throat. 'It was...crowded,' she said defensively, dropping her hands and folding her arms primly.

Tuck's gaze dropped. Her folded arms had pushed her breasts up and together, exposing a nice curve of bare flesh at the criss-cross front of her dress for his viewing pleasure. Tuck had seen a lot bigger. He'd also seen smaller. Cassie's looked just about right to him. A perky B cup, he'd hazard a guess.

Tuck grinned. 'Come on, darlin', it's late. Let's get you to bed.'

Cassie shoved her hands on her hips, determined not to let an image of him sprawled in her big hotel bed derail her thoughts. 'Don't call me *darlin'*.' She mimicked his slow, easy Southern drawl to perfection. 'And I'm perfectly capable of finding my way to my room. *I* can count.'

Tuck's grin broadened. 'Well, maybe you can help me find my room?' He scratched his head in the most perplexed manner he could muster. 'There's a lot of wings in this place and it does get kind of confusin' after a hundred, don't it?'

Cassie rolled her eyes. The man was living proof that evolution could go in reverse. 'How on earth do you count all those millions that kicking a stupid ball around earned you?'

Tuck shoved his hands in his pockets. 'Got me some bean-counters for that.'

Cassie couldn't believe what she was hearing. He was going to be one of those has-been sports stars whose money was all gone in a matter of years because he had a little too much yardage between the goalposts to keep track of it himself. And he trusted too easily.

'Follow me,' she said huffily as she headed down the long grand hallway.

Tuck's gaze ran over the contours of her back and settled on how her dress swung and fluttered with each movement. 'Your wish is my command,' he murmured under his breath.

Tuck deliberately took his time, stopping to examine old paintings hanging on the stonework, suits of armour and the antique vases that dotted the magnificent corridor. He kept up a running commentary for Cassie's sake, purely because it seemed to annoy her.

'*Will* you hurry up?' she said impatiently, looking over her shoulder for the tenth time as he stopped to read the name of the artist of a particularly austere portrait. 'I have a paper to get to.'

Tuck looked up. 'You brought work?' He shook his head at her and tsked as he meandered closer. 'All work and no play makes Cassiopeia a dull girl.'

Cassie glared at him as they got underway again. 'Not that I expect you to understand this, but there is nothing dull about auroras on Jupiter.'

'Auroras?'

'Yes—you know, like the Aurora Borealis?' His blank look didn't seem promising. 'The Northern Lights?' she clarified.

Tuck had witnessed the Aurora Borealis in Scandinavia on two separate occasions, but he wasn't about to disappoint Cassie's assumptions. 'Isn't she some mermaid?'

Cassie sighed. There really *was* no grain in his silo. He

was an empty vessel. 'No. It's a *real* thing. It's why I'm here. I'm completing my PhD studies at Cornell so next year I can go on a research trip to Antarctica. And Aurora was Sleeping Beauty. *Ariel* was the Little Mermaid.'

Tuck shrugged. 'Well, it sounds like a mermaid if you ask me.' And then he shot her his best goofy grin for good measure.

Thankfully her room approached, and Cassie all but leapt at the ornate doorknob. 'This is me,' she said. 'What did you say your room number was again?'

She'd barely been able to concentrate on anything he'd said. When he wasn't wandering off like a distracted child or lagging behind to look at things he was right there beside her, weaving his heady scent all around her.

Like he was now.

Tuck smiled. 'Three hundred and twenty three,' he said, and watched the fact that he would be sleeping directly opposite her dawn slowly on her face. 'Howdy, neighbour.'

'Oh.' Cassie looked at the door opposite. Too close for comfort. Her highly developed sense of fight or flight kicked in as another dose of his masculinity wafted over her.

'Right, then,' she said, fishing in Gina's glittery clutch purse for her room key and locating it with shaking hands.

The adrenaline. It had to be the adrenaline.

'Goodnight,' she said, barely looking at him as she turned away and reached for the door handle, hastily swiping the plastic card through the electronic strip.

The light turned red and she swiped it again, her

hands even shakier. Another red light elicited a frustrated little growl from the back of her throat. She needed to get inside her room. Inside was work and logic and focus and sanity.

Out here with Tuck's quiet presence behind her was insanity. *And damnation.*

She could feel it pulling at her body with sticky tentacles, drugging her with its perfume, wrapping her up in its heady thrall.

She swiped one more time. *Red light.*

'Allow me.'

Cassie's fingers stilled as Tuck's hand slid over them. His body moved in behind hers and she was instantly cocooned in his intoxicating aroma. She shut her eyes as her nipples responded to the blatant cue. She could feel his breath in her hair, the warm press of his chest against her back, the power of his thighs behind hers.

She leant her forehead against the door, desperately reaching for logic. 'I spend all day probing the outer depths of our solar system through a massive telescope,' she said. 'I'm pretty sure I can open a damn door.'

'Shh,' Tuck said, easing the key out of her unresisting fingers. 'Some things don't need big brains,' he murmured. He took the plastic. 'Some things need a slow hand...an easy touch.'

He slid the card through the strip with deliberate slowness. The lock whirred, the light turned green and he smiled as he turned the handle and pushed the door open a fraction.

'Easy.'

Cassie practically whimpered at the low, deep sound

of his Southern accent. It weaved around her like the melodic notes of a snake charmer, trapping her. The door was right there. It was open. All she needed to do was move. But she couldn't.

'Cassie?'

Tuck could feel her trembling and a surge of desire crested in his belly. His groin tightened. His blood slowed to a thick, primal bound. He laid a gentle hand on her shoulder and, to his surprise, she turned. Only a whisper separated them as heat flashed like a solar flare between them.

Her eyes looked all misty and dazed, her pupils large in the grey-blue depths. They seemed to shimmer up at him and he fell headlong into them. Her mouth was slightly parted and it drew his gaze. He picked up a long dark ringlet draped forward over her shoulder and wound it around his finger. 'Has anyone ever told you you're quite beautiful?'

Cassie's throat was dry as a sandpit as she shut her eyes against the seduction in his. No one had ever told her that. And she'd never cared. 'I've never aspired to be beautiful,' she dismissed. She was more comfortable with brainy.

He waited for her lashes to flutter open again before saying, 'Well, you've failed.'

Tuck only intended to give her the briefest of kisses as he slid his palm onto her cheek. Just a little taste of her mouth. The mouth that had dissed him all night. Just to show her how pretty damn clever he could be.

And to leave her wanting more.

But the second his mouth touched hers and she

opened to him as if he was water and she was dying of thirst it all went flying out of the window.

Cassie mewed as his lips brushed hers and her senses filled up with him. There was no thought or logic or analysis in play any longer as she overdosed on his intoxicating scent, sucking him in, drenching her cells in his pheromones. Her body had completely taken over and left her brain out of the equation.

She raised herself up on tiptoes. Her hands slid around his neck. Her mouth parted of its own accord. She moaned and dragged him closer as hot, scalding lust lashed her insides and flayed her flesh with the driving need for more.

It didn't make any sense. Not when she swiped her tongue across his lips, or pushed it inside, or stroked it against his. Not when she moaned. Not when she gasped. Not when she grabbed his lapels to press herself closer.

She'd never been kissed like this.

She'd never *kissed* like this.

And still she was full of him. Her head buzzed with the essence of him. Her mouth was on fire. Her belly was tight. The heat between her legs tingled and burned.

Tuck barely managed to hold onto her as Cassie kissed him as if she was an evil genius intent on wicked things and he was her latest experiment. He might not be dumb as a rock but he was certainly as hard as one now as her deep, sexy kisses, body-squirming and desperate little whimpers stroked all his hot spots.

She even kissed differently from other women. No mouth gymnastics, no hands down his pants in seconds, no theatrical panting, no *Oh, baby, baby*. Just a scorching one hundred percent, full-throttle touchdown of a kiss. Her lips on his lips. Open and going for it.

He pushed her hard against the door, wanting to get closer, to kiss her deeper. But he'd forgotten it was already slightly open and she stumbled backwards. Their mouths tore apart.

He grabbed for her, finding her elbow, dropping it once she'd stabilised. And then they stood staring at each other, breathing hard, not moving for a moment, neither sure which way to jump.

Tuck knew enough about women to know that look in Cassie's eyes. He knew he could pick her up, stride into her room and lay her on the bed and she'd follow wherever he took her. And enjoy every single second of it.

But he saw a whole bunch of other stuff in her eyes too. Most of it he couldn't decipher. But he could see her confusion quite clearly. Obviously that kiss just did not compute for Cassie.

She looked as if she needed some time to wrap her head around it. Hell, *he* sure as hell did!

'Are you okay?'

Cassie nodded automatically *but* she doubted she'd ever be okay again. *What the hell had just happened?* She felt as if she'd just had a lobotomy. Could a kiss render you stupid?

'I think I should go now. Unless...' He dropped his gaze to her swollen mouth.

Cassie shook her head and took a step back. *No 'unless'. Go, yes. Just go.* He'd turned her into a dunce.

Tuck smiled at her dazed look. It was nice to have left an impression on Little-Miss-Know-It-All, even if he *was* going to go to bed with a hard-on the size of Texas. 'Goodnight, Cassiopeia.'

Cassie was incapable of answering him. She feared she'd been struck mute. As well as dumb. She watched him swagger to his room opposite, slot his key in, open his door. He turned as he stepped into his room.

'I'll be right over here. If you need a cup of *shhu-gar*.'

Cassie had no pithy comeback as his door clicked quietly shut.

THREE

AFTER TOSSING AND turning for most of the night—not something that was good for her sanity—Cassie woke at nine a.m. and the first thing she thought about was Tuck. She dragged a pillow over her head and bellowed a loud, furious denial.

She *always* woke at six. And most certainly *never* thought about a man.

Cassie's brain was engaged the moment her eyes flicked open after her regulation eight hours' sleep. For the last several years her waking thoughts had centred on her aurora research and she'd spring out of bed and head straight for her computer.

This morning her head was full of Tuck and *the kiss*.

Her computer, the research, *her will to live*—all lost in a sea of oestrogen.

She yanked the pillow off her head and turned on her side. Her baggy T-shirt was twisted around her torso and the movement pulled it taut against her breasts. Her nipples responded to the brush of fabric, her belly clamped, and a red-hot tingle took up residence at the juncture of her thighs.

Cassie dragged some deep breaths in and out, trying to conjure up the latest deep-space images she'd seen yesterday. But it was no use—she could still smell him in her nostrils and taste him on her mouth.

The phone rang and she snatched it up immediately, grateful for something else to do, to think about.

'Hello?'

'Cassie, get off that computer and get your heiny down here now,' Marnie demanded. 'Reese is back and we're having breakfast.'

Her friend's Southern accent reminded her of Tuck's lazy Texan drawl and Cassie almost groaned out loud. 'I'll be there in ten.'

Anything—*anything*—to take her mind off the annoying jock.

Cassie entered the grand dining room exactly ten minutes later, completely oblivious to the eyebrows her rather informal attire was raising. She'd thrown on a pair of loose leggings and a baggy T-shirt with a slogan that said *'Back in my day we had nine planets'*—one of the many geek-themed shirts Gina, Marnie and Reese had sent her over the years.

She hadn't even bothered to brush her hair—just pulled it back into her regulation low ponytail, with her regulation floral scrunchie, and pushed one of her many-toothed Alice bands into it, ensuring it stayed scraped back off her forehead. There really was nothing more annoying than hair getting in the way when she was in the middle of something.

Actually, there was now. And its name was *Tuck*.

Unlike the rest of the people in the dining room, dressed in their country club pastels, her friends didn't bat an eyelid as Cassie scurried their way, then plonked herself in one of the three empty seats at the round table. They'd have been shocked had Cassie dressed in any other way.

Cassie forced a smile to her face as she looked at a glowing Reese, radiating the same kind of happiness she had a decade ago when she and her Marine had first met. 'When did you get back? Where's Mason?'

'An hour ago.' Reese grinned, sipping at some coffee. 'He's taking care of some business.'

Cassie barely registered Reese's reply but nodded anyway. A waiter interrupted and Cassie, ignoring the piles of pancakes the others were tucking into, ordered the same thing she had every morning for breakfast—yoghurt and muesli and two slices of grain toast with Vegemite. When he informed her they didn't have Vegemite she ordered jam.

'You okay?' Reese frowned. 'You look kind of tired.'

'I didn't sleep very well,' Cassie said.

Marnie looked at Gina, and Gina narrowed her eyes at Cassie. 'Since when doesn't Little-Miss-Eight-Hours not sleep well?'

Cassie looked at her friends all watching her with curiosity. She shrugged. She didn't know what to tell them because she'd *never* not slept well.

Gina lounged back in her chair, her arms crossed, her

fingers tapping against her arms. 'This hasn't got anything to do with a certain quarterback, has it?'

Marnie sat forward, her blonde hair neat as a pin in a high ponytail that was one hundred percent more cute and perky than Cassie's. 'It does, doesn't it?'

Reese frowned at both her friends. 'Tuck?'

'Tuck and Cassie danced last night,' Gina said.

'Real close,' Marnie added.

Reese blinked at her. 'Cassie?'

Cassie had decided on her way down to the dining room that she wasn't going to tell a soul about the strange feelings coursing through her body, but she felt herself sag under the scrutiny of three sets of eyes. She'd always been a great believer in solving problems by seeking out experts in the field. And, having lived with these three women and been through all their relationship ups and downs, she had to admit she had a panel of experts in front of her.

What better people to confide in?

'I don't know what's happening,' she murmured. 'I couldn't sleep last night. I *always* sleep. I *need* to sleep. It's vitally important that I do. I take *specific* medication to switch off my brain so I can sleep. And it never fails. I'm out like a light. Usually... And this morning I didn't wake until nine... I'm always up at six. *Always.*'

'Well, you were tired,' Marnie reasoned.

'And do you know what my first waking thought was about?' Cassie continued, ignoring Marnie.

'I'm guessing it was about something a little closer to the earth than usual?' Gina said.

Cassie sighed in disgust. 'It was him. *The jock.*' She

looked at her friends for answers. 'I don't understand what's happening to me.'

Her friends didn't say anything for a moment, as if they were waiting for her to say more or to clarify something. Then, one by one, the three women opposite her broke into broad grins.

She frowned. 'What?'

Her friends had the audacity to laugh then, looking at each other as they cracked up. Cassie glared at them. 'This is not funny.'

'No, of course not,' Reese soothed as she struggled to regain her composure. 'Falling in love is never funny.'

Cassie gaped at Reese. 'Don't be ridiculous,' she spluttered.

'Aww...' Marnie purred, ignoring Cassie's protest. 'Our little girl is all grown up now,' she teased.

'And to think,' Reese continued, 'we voted you the girl least likely to ever fall for a man.'

Cassie crossed her arms across her chest and waited for their frivolity to wane. She would not entertain such unscientific mumbo-jumbo. Love was a fiction perpetuated by romance novels and Hollywood.

'It's not love,' she said frostily when the last smile had fallen beneath her uncompromising glare. 'Just because you're seeing the world through rose-coloured glasses, Reese, does not mean I've taken leave of *my* senses. You know I don't believe in that voodoo. It's his pheromones—that's all. The man smells *incredible*...'

Cassie could still smell him on her, and she shut her eyes for a moment to savour it.

'It was dizzying,' she said, eyes still closed. 'Truly sensational. Like it was all I could do to stop myself sniffing and sniffing and sniffing him all night.'

Cassie's eyelids fluttered open and she found her friends staring at her with varying degrees of perplexity. She cleared her throat and straightened in her chair. 'Anyway...it's obviously a scent I'm biologically programmed to respond to. It's just...biochemistry. Nothing more.'

The waiter arrived and conversation stopped as he placed Cassie's breakfast in front of her. When he left Cassie looked at Gina. 'Surely there's a lay word for that other than *love*? When your body overrules your brain?'

Gina nodded. 'Yep. We call it horny.'

Cassie shook her head. 'No.' She was a scientist. *She refused to be horny.*

Gina nodded again. 'Totally gagging for it.'

Cassie wasn't sure what that meant exactly, but it sounded like something they'd say in the locker room on an American cop show. 'Absolutely not.'

'Libido?' Reese supplied.

Cassie paused. She liked that word best. It was backed up by science—the non-Freudian kind. It could be proved—the area of the brain responsible for libido had been studied extensively.

'Yes,' Gina agreed. 'It's your libido knocking.'

'Okay, I can buy that,' Cassie conceded. 'But my libido has never been an issue before, so why is it knocking now?'

'Well, that's easy,' Gina said. 'When was the last time you had sex?'

Cassie thought about it for a moment. It had been Len's birthday request. 'Seven months ago.'

Gina blinked. 'Seven *months?*' She looked at Reese and Marnie, who were also staring at Cassie's admission. 'Well, in that case it's *definitely* your libido.'

'Who's the guy?' Marnie asked.

'His name is Len. He's another astronomer at the university. We've been working on the same project for the last five years. We have a regular hook-up.'

'Every *seven* months?' Gina interjected.

'It varies,' Cassie said, oblivious to the palpable incredulity around the table. 'Usually whenever he starts to get cranky. I've found that it improves his focus.'

'Okay...' Gina said, shaking her head. 'So this last time—was it...you know...good?'

Cassie shrugged. Personally she'd never got the big deal about sex. 'It was satisfactory.'

Gina looked at Reese for back-up. 'I think what Gina means,' Reese continued, 'is did you...you know...' she lowered her voice '...orgasm?'

'Oh, no,' Cassie said, unfazed by the conversation. When they'd all lived together Cassie had been privy to many girly chats about all kinds of sex-related issues. She'd learned a great deal of stuff in that house that a bunch of lectures and books had never taught her. 'I've never had an orgasm.'

Had Cassie been one to find humour in awkward situations she would have found the total disbelief on her friends' faces completely hilarious. They'd all stopped eating and were staring at her.

'What...*never?*' Marnie asked after a stunned silence.

Cassie shook her head. 'No.'

'Not even…by yourself?' Reese asked.

'Or with a vibrator?' added Gina, last to recover.

Cassie looked from one to the other. 'I've never masturbated and I don't own, nor have I ever, a vibrator.'

More silence followed, finally broken by Gina's, 'Well, that's just *unnatural*. Going without sex is one thing, but there is no excuse for not indulging in a little self-love, Cassiopeia. It's perfectly healthy. *Normal*, actually. Didn't I teach you anything?'

Cassie put down her spoon. 'No, it's fine. Some people don't need sex.' She shrugged. 'I'm one of them.'

'It's *not* fine,' Reese interjected. 'I don't know who this Len is that you've been having sex with…very, *very* infrequently…but he's definitely doing it all wrong.'

'No, it's not his fault.'

'Oh, I think it is,' Marnie said.

'No, really.' Cassie looked at her friends' concerned faces. 'The medication I take to sleep…one of its side-effects is libido suppression and difficulty achieving orgasm.'

Gina shuddered. 'I think I'd rather stay awake for the rest of my life.' She looked at Cassie. 'Are you sure you need it?'

Cassie nodded. 'Without it my brain doesn't switch off and I can't sleep. And that's extremely detrimental to my health. I start to get a little OCD without sleep. And one stay in the psych ward as a teenager was more than enough.' Cassie vividly remembered the chaos her mind had descended into—how she'd quickly spiralled out of control. 'Trust me, that's an experience I never want to repeat.'

Gina, Reese and Marnie didn't even know what to say to *that* revelation. They were still stuck back at the no-orgasm thing.

'I still think Len could try a little harder,' Marnie said after the silence had gone on for a while.

'Oh, he tried in the beginning. A couple of times. But it wasn't happening and it was taking for ever and I really don't have time for all that carry-on. It was never really for my benefit anyway, so now we don't bother about me.'

Gina gaped. 'Do you...kiss? Is there foreplay?'

Cassie shook her head. 'Not really. I prefer it when he cuts to the chase. It's quicker that way.'

Gina looked at Reese. 'Where did we go wrong with her?'

Reese shook her head. 'I have no idea.'

'Right,' Gina said, picking up her coffee cup and taking a sip. 'Let's deal with the most pressing issue and hopefully the other problem will sort itself out. What we have here is you suffering from a libido that has suddenly roared to life—which is probably due to a combination of lack of sexual satisfaction for the *entirety* of your life and the fact that you're almost thirty. Women's sex drives peak around thirty. That's a well-known scientific fact, right? Or it is according to women's magazines.'

Cassie nodded. 'Correct.'

'And Tuck has come along at this crossroads of sexual frustration and the natural peaking of your sex drive and it's like he's...tripped a switch.'

Cassie was pretty sure it could be put more scientifically, but she liked Gina's logic. And logic was beautiful. 'Good. Okay. So what do I do about it?'

Gina shrugged, putting her coffee cup back in its saucer. 'Easy. You bonk Tuck's brains out until that libido of yours stops bitching.'

Reese choked on a mouthful of pancake. When she'd finished coughing she said to Gina, 'I don't think that's a good idea. I love my cousin. He's hot and sweet, and from what I read in the tabloids he may well be God's gift to the female of the species, but he's not exactly the settling down type.'

'I'm not suggesting she *marry* the man,' Gina said. 'Not *everyone* needs to get married, Reese.' She turned to look at Cassie. 'I think she should just use him for sex—get him out of her system. He doesn't look like the kind of man who'd object to being used as a scratching post for a horny thirty-year-old genius.'

Cassie felt something tighten low and deep inside her at the mere thought of being horizontal with Tuck. 'Maybe I could just up my meds? Suppress my libido chemically?'

Marnie reached out her hand and placed it over top of Cassie's. 'There could be worse ways to iron out a few kinks, Cass. He's a mighty fine-looking man. Very sexy.'

Cassie was pretty sure there weren't. Why did her body want *him*? Mighty fine or not, the man had clearly forgotten to pay his brain bill. What on earth were they going to talk about while they were *doing* it? She and Len discussed their research. What could she talk to *him* about?

'Yeah, but I'm not sure I want to be naked in front of a guy who doesn't know what Pi is... Why couldn't he be a geek? Smart men are my kind of sexy.'

Reese shook her head. 'He played dumb, didn't he?' she said to Gina.

'Yep. To be fair, though,' Gina said, 'Cassie *was* speaking to him slowly and using very simple words.'

Reese sighed. 'Yeah, he does that when people make assumptions.' She looked at Cassie. 'Well, you better hold on to your hat, Cassiopeia, because Tuck's brain is about as big as his ego. He graduated *summa cum laude* in pure math and he's currently working with a young start-up company in California developing a stats app for the NFL. He's no savant, but he's no dummy either.'

It was Cassie's turn to blink. 'Maths?' She *loved* maths.

Reese nodded. 'Not just a pretty face.'

Marnie straightened up. 'Speaking of pretty faces....'

Gina and Reese also straightened. 'What?' Cassie turned to look behind her. Not that she really needed to. She could already feel his pull.

She sucked in a breath as Tuck swaggered towards them, once again greeting his fans with casual aplomb. Was it his broad chest and narrow hips, beautifully showcased in dark trousers and a pale lemon shirt unbuttoned at the throat, that flared her nostrils and set her mouth watering? Or maybe it was his short crinkly blond locks that would surely curl with any kind of length?

Or was it just his big beautiful brain that made her want to lick him all over? *Dear God, she was turning into an animal!*

Cassie quickly turned back, her brain already shutting down. Reese glanced at Gina and Marnie, who were both watching Cassie's reaction with bemused expressions. They'd seen their friend flustered before—but never over a man.

'Morning, ladies,' Tuck said as he drew within a metre of the table. 'Cassiopeia,' he murmured as he pulled up the chair beside her and sat down.

He turned to smile at her. Except Cassie this morning was very different from the one last night. Her hair was straight and ruthlessly pushed off her face, her make-up was non-existent, and she was wearing something baggy and voluminous that totally obscured the body she'd been showing off last night.

She was no swan this morning, that was for sure.

But her pretty grey-blue eyes still looked at him with that compelling mix of intelligence and confusion and he liked that he was still rattling her.

'You turn into a pumpkin, darlin'?'

'Tuck!' Reese gasped.

'What?' he protested, looking at his cousin completely unabashed. 'I'm just saying Cassie's looking a little...different this morning.'

Cassie wasn't remotely insulted by the observation. How she looked or didn't look had never mattered. What concerned her was the riot going on inside her body as his scent, now encoded into her DNA, pulled her into its orbit. The sudden leap in her pulse, the flare of her nostrils, the gush of saliva coating a mouth as dry as stardust.

He smelled different this morning, but the same.

There was a hint of something sweet, a tang masking the earthy smell of male, but it only added to his allure. It tickled at her nose with each inhalation. It wafted over her in sticky waves. It undulated through her breasts and belly.

She could see the hollow at the base of his throat, the steady bound of his pulse, and it took all her willpower to stop herself leaning into him and burying her nose right there.

Dear God—he might not be as stupid as she'd thought, but she was losing IQ points fast.

Everyone was looking at her. *Say something, damn it!*

'Why, when you have a maths degree, did you lead me to believe you were dumb?'

Tuck shot a look at his cousin. 'Aww, Reese,' he said, putting on his best yokel accent, 'you done went and spoiled all my fun.'

'Knock it off, Tuck.' Reese tutted. 'You shouldn't bait people. It's not nice.'

Cassie frowned, ignoring them. 'I don't understand why you would underestimate your intelligence.'

Tuck supposed Cassie wouldn't, in her world of logic and reason, so there was no point trying to explain how crazy being treated like a dumb jock made him. She hadn't been deliberately obtuse, like so many others, just clueless, so he was prepared to cut her some slack.

'Would you have let me kiss you some more last night if you'd known I was smarter?'

Cassie suspected she very much would have. Brains and pheromones were apparently a dangerous combination. Hell, the man could kiss her right now, in front of a dining room full of people, and she'd be powerless to resist.

'Some more?' Gina said, her eyebrows practically hitting her hairline.

'He kissed you!' Marnie spluttered.

'You kissed her?' Reese demanded.

Tuck looked at the three fierce women opposite him and then at the silent one beside him, her gaze roving over his throat like a vampire deciding where to make her first bite. It branded him like a physical caress and streaked heat to his groin where things stirred with the same potency they'd had last night.

'Cassie?' Marnie prompted.

Cassie dragged her eyes off Tuck's neck. 'Oh, yeah. I left that bit out, didn't I?'

'Er, *yeah*,' Marnie said.

Cassie looked at her friends, all looking at her expectantly, waiting for more. Tuck was watching her too. And all the while his pheromones battered and pulled at her, weakening her resistance. She had to get away from them.

From him.

She stood. 'I have work to do.'

'Oh, no—wait, Cassie,' Marnie said. 'You can't spend all your time at a luxury estate holed up in your room on your laptop.'

Tuck couldn't agree more. Being holed up in her room with her on his lap, making Little-Miss-Know-It-All come undone, sounded much preferable.

'Marnie's right,' Gina said. 'We're going to the spa for the day. Why don't you join us?'

Cassie was surprised that Marnie and Gina were voluntarily spending time in each other's company. Although was that a desperate *please come* look in Gina's eyes? Normally she would have agreed to be their buffer zone, but a day where their deflection would land squarely on her and, by association, Tuck, was not something she wanted to volunteer for.

Gina might be convinced that *bonking* Tuck was the solution, but Cassie wasn't ready to allow hormones and libido to conquer brainpower.

She just needed to get absorbed in her work again.

'Stars wait for no woman,' she said, glancing at Tuck for good measure, to send him a message too—*she wouldn't be derailed by biology.*

And she fell into his cosmic blue eyes, temporarily forgetting her own name.

Tuck smiled at her, raising an eyebrow slightly at her defiant expression. But she wasn't fooling him. He could see other things in her gaze as well, like the hunger from last night. Maybe he could convince her about the beauty of a different kind of star. The kind that popped and exploded behind shut lids as she rode the tail of a stratospheric orgasm.

'Join us later for something to eat.'

Cassie dragged her gaze from Tuck's, grateful to Gina for the interruption. He looked at her as if he knew exactly what she was thinking and it was unsettling. 'I'll see,' she evaded as Gina's desperation not to be alone with Marnie was confirmed. 'I have a lot of stuff to get through before I start at Cornell next week. I'll probably get room service.'

She might not be looking at him but she could still feel his eyes on her. His words from last night came back to her. *All work and no play make Cassie a dull girl.* She'd never been tempted to ditch her work before, but his hot gaze made her want to do a lot of things she hadn't done.

'We'll call you when we're done,' Marnie said.

Cassie nodded. She stood awkwardly for a moment or two, conscious of all eyes on her, then bade them goodbye.

The four remaining occupants of the table watched her walk away. Tuck shuddered as her shapeless shirt hung like a bag on her frame.

'Now, why would a woman want to hide such a damn fine figure?' he asked as he turned back to face the table.

Three sets of female eyes were trained firmly upon him and he shifted uncomfortably. He was a man used to female attention—but not like this.

'What?' he said warily.

'Don't play with her, Tuck,' Reese warned. 'She's not like your other women.'

Tuck kind of liked that the most about Cassie, but he cocked an eyebrow and tried to look a little insulted. 'My other women?'

'You know what I mean,' Reese said reproachfully. 'She's not a player.'

'She's pretty sheltered,' Marnie added.

Tuck looked at Cassie's three musketeers. 'She's a big girl. Surely she can look after herself?'

'She's not experienced with guys like you,' Gina explained.

'Guys like me?'

Gina shot him a silky smile. 'Man-whore guys.'

Tuck faked a hurt look and shot it his cousin's way. 'Reese, honey, your friends are being mean to me.'

Reese snorted. 'Tuck. Listen to me. I know your career ending in injury the way it did was hard, and that you've been a little aimless since your divorce and have been... enjoying the spoils of being God's gift to women...but I'm asking you to *not* choose Cassie as your next form of denial.'

It was Tuck's turn to snort. His career ending, his impulsive marriage crumbling, his infertility—all had been body-blows over the last couple of years. Separately they would have been challenging to any man's ego, but together they'd been an enormous whammy. So what if he'd been trying to prove he was still *the man?*

But Reese was right, Cassie wasn't his type. He dated women who knew the ropes. And he didn't need a PhD in relationships to know that Cassie did not.

He put up his hands in surrender. 'Okay. I won't go near her. I promise.'

Reese patted his hand. 'Atta-boy.'

By ten o'clock Cassie was ready to weep with frustration. She'd achieved exactly nothing all day. Instead of auroras and how they affected weather patterns on Jupiter she'd doodled Tuck's name on a writing pad all day. Every web search she'd conducted, every paper she'd picked up, every image she'd looked at, Tuck and his smell and his accent and his lazy grin had hijacked her thoughts.

Her whole body ached with trying to deny the surge of

hormones that had her in their thrall. Two cold showers hadn't helped—she still felt hot and feverish, as if she was craving a drug. She'd tried to work through it, she really had, but everything got back to Tuck.

One night—that was all she had to do. She just had to get through this night and then she'd be gone in the morning, and far away from him and his pheromones, and she could get her brain back. Her focus.

She stared at her door for the thousandth time. Just through it and across the hallway was the cause of all her angst. Cassie took a step towards it. *No!* She forced herself to stop, turn around. She snatched up the phone instead and dialled Gina.

'I need you to talk me off the ledge.'

'Well, hello to you too,' Gina said.

'I mean it. I can't stop thinking about him.'

'If you rang me to talk you out of it, you rang the wrong friend—should have chosen Marnie. I absolutely think you should go for it.'

Cassie gripped the phone. Suddenly she *was* ready for hormones and libido to trump brainpower. 'Tell me more about your theory.'

'What...the bonk Tuck theory?'

'Yes.'

'It's simple, really. You're the one who's always telling us we're biological creatures at heart, with primal needs, right?'

'Uh-huh.'

'So isn't it logical, then, to follow that biological imperative?'

Cassie liked logic—a lot. And she couldn't fault Gina's.

She'd just never imagined that *she'd* be at the mercy of biology.

'Look upon it as an experiment to prove the theory,' Gina continued. 'You scientists are big on that, right? You have a problem. Tuck could be the solution. But there's only one way to find out for sure, right?'

'So like a...a sexual experiment?'

'Yes,' Gina said enthusiastically. 'Exactly.'

'I guess I could submit to a one-off experiment,' Cassie mused, chewing her lip, her heart pounding at the thought. 'To test the theory.'

'Er...it might take more than a one-off, Cass.'

Cassie considered that for a moment. 'I don't think so. I don't think I'm wired for more than one-offs...and it's about biology after all, right? So, theoretically, the act of copulation should be enough to satisfy.'

'I think you're going to get more than *copulation* from Tuck. Just saying...'

Cassie nodded, ignoring the warning as her brain moved on to logistics. 'So, what...? I should just go up and say *How about it?*'

Gina laughed. 'Just knock on his door and tell him you want him. Trust me, he'll take it from there.'

Tuck glanced at the clock when a knock sounded on his door. It was almost eleven. He was sprawled on his king-size bed, in his hotel robe, watching a game with the lights and the sound turned low.

And he knew it was her.

He drained the last of his beer before sauntering towards the door, a grin on his face. He turned the handle and pulled it partially open, his hand sliding up the frame to rest somewhere above his head.

Cassie stood there looking up at him. 'Can I come in?'

Tuck felt her quiet request grab hold of his gut and squeeze. No sexy posturing. No batting of her eyelids. 'What do you want, Cassiopeia?'

Cassie swallowed, not even sure if she could get the word out around her parched throat. 'You,' she croaked.

Tuck's breath stuttered to a halt for a moment and his grip on the door tightened. She was grim-faced and serious, and sporting scraped-back hair and terrible clothes, yet his body surged to attention. He'd promised he wouldn't go near her, but he hadn't made any promises in regards to her coming to *him*.

He pulled the door open further and fell back, gesturing her inside.

FOUR

_____

CASSIE SHUT HER eyes as she brushed past him, her nostrils flaring at his scent, her dry mouth suddenly inundated with saliva. She walked to the centre of the room, her heart rate ratcheting off the charts. She turned to face him. He was lounging against the door, and in the dim light he looked all broad and brooding and watchful.

Now what?

She'd kind of hoped he'd take over from here. Gina had assured her he would. But clearly he wasn't going to make it easy.

'Are you going to stand over there?' she asked.

Her voice sounded weird in the air-conditioned bubble of the silent hotel room. High and breathy. She swallowed again.

'For the moment,' Tuck said, crossing his arms.

Cassie wished he wouldn't. She wanted him to come closer. To bring his height and his breadth and his perfectly symmetrical features and his incredibly male smell right over, close to her. And take the lead.

Computing the wind speed across auroras on giant gas planets, she could do—asking a man to have sex with her, not so much.

She opened her mouth, took a tentative step towards him, then stopped. Shut her mouth. This should be easy. A cinch. She had a giant brain and an excellent vocabulary. But once again she felt as if she was wearing the dunce's cap.

Tuck took pity on her. He'd never known a woman to be alone in a room with him and *not* know what to do. Especially when he was in nothing but a robe and his underwear. It was strangely erotic.

'So, does "*you*" mean what I think it means?' he asked.

Cassie's brain came back online at the verbal prompt. He was giving her a way in—a conversation-starter. And she snatched at it like the last molecule of oxygen on earth.

'Yes,' she said, then cleared her throat because it sounded sappy and weak again. 'I'm not very good at this—'

'Boy,' Tuck interrupted with a smile, 'how'd that one go down? Couldn't have been easy to admit. I imagine you're good at most things.'

Cassie glared at his interruption—didn't he know how hard this was? 'I'm good at *everything*...except this.'

'And *this* is...?'

Cassie took a deep breath. 'This is me asking you to have sex. With me.'

It was blunt and gauche and totally unsexy—and Tuck had never been more turned on in his life.

'This is purely scientific, you understand?' Cassie

clarified as Tuck continued to watch her with his blue eyes. 'I seem to have developed a...thing for your pheromones.'

Tuck raised an eyebrow. 'My pheromones?'

'Yes. They're chemicals the body emits—'

Tuck chuckled, interrupting her. 'I know what pheromones are, Cassiopeia.'

'Oh, right...yes, sorry. Well, I don't know if you know this or not, but you do smell pretty amazing.'

Tuck smiled. 'I have been told that a time or two before.'

Cassie absorbed that information, missing the nuance in her bid to get to the point. 'Anyway...I find myself unable to concentrate on my work, and Gina suggested that, because I'm a female in my sexual prime, my libido is demanding to be...serviced...and that a spot of...copulation...might be the solution to my problem.'

Tuck felt his erection swell further. He should *not* be turned on by a woman in shapeless clothes talking about servicing and copulation. Pretty, perky women with enhanced assets and bold use of four-letter words were his staple turn-ons.

And yet he was very turned on. 'Copulation?'

She nodded. 'It's all very logical, really.'

Tuck made his way towards her, keeping his pace slow and lazy. 'So this is you *seducing* me?'

Cassie took a step back as his masculine scent drew her into his wild pheromone cloud. 'I...guess.'

Tuck stopped when he was an arm's length from her. He dropped his gaze and took a slow tour of her body. It didn't take long—there wasn't a lot he could make out.

Her breasts, which he remembered very well from her criss-cross dress last night, were vaguely discernible beneath a voluminous T-shirt that proclaimed *'Come to the nerd side. We have Pi'*.

He smiled at the logo as he lifted a hand and fingered the sleeve. *'This* is what you wear to a seduction?'

Cassie looked down. It hadn't even occurred to her to change her clothes. She'd got into her pyjamas an hour ago, after her second cold shower. Gina would have a fit if she knew. 'Oh. Yes. Guess it's not very—' she swallowed '—sexy.'

Tuck shrugged. 'Funny can be sexy.'

'It's a tradition,' she explained as his gaze roved all over her shirt. It suddenly felt like it was on fire. 'Gina, Reese and Marnie send me geek T-shirts as a...it's a joke...' She petered out as she realised she was babbling. 'Sorry. Like I say, I'm not very good at this.'

Tuck disagreed. Cassie's unique approach was being very much appreciated by one particular part of his body. 'So,' he murmured, his fingers dropping from Cassie's sleeve to stroke up and down her arm, 'would you like the standard copulation package or one of the many variations I offer?'

Cassie pulled her arm away as an army of goose bumps marched across her skin and a seductive waft of Tuck flared her nostrils. 'Oh, I think the standard will be fine.' Her voice was husky again and she cleared it. 'I still have a paper to get back to. No time for variations.'

Tuck smiled. A man with a less robust ego might have been intimidated by her haste to be done with it. But he was not one to go for *'copulation'* by the clock. And she'd given him a goal now—to wipe that research paper from her head for the rest of the night.

Or die trying.

'Okay,' he said, stepping in closer to her, until her body was a hand-touch away, 'long, sweet, slow loving it is.'

Cassie swayed as her senses were engulfed in a wave of him, drenching every cell in a primal urge. She felt his hand warm on her waist, steadying her, and her eyes pinged open, her gaze snared in the brilliant blue of his.

'That's your *standard*?' she asked, her voice squeaky.

Tuck shrugged. 'I have high standards.'

He brought his free hand up to cradle her jaw. Her pupils were large and dilated, the sound of her breath was rough in his ears, her nostrils were flaring, her mouth was parted. Tuck knew all the signs of an aroused woman. And any other woman would be plastered all over him by now, eager to fulfil his every whim.

The fact that she wasn't was sweet and quaint and endearing. And vaguely thrilling.

Not that he had any issues with sexually aggressive women. He loved confidence and strength in and out of bed. But this—having a woman waiting for *his* move for a change—was, strangely, a real turn-on.

Cassie swore she could hear the sluggish grind of gears as time seemed to slow right down. Her head spun with the smell of him and she wanted him to kiss her so badly she didn't even recognise the woman she'd suddenly become.

'Tuck...' The word spilled from her lips on a desperate whisper she had no conscious control over.

Tuck sucked in a breath. The volume of want in her voice was lashing him with an identical desire. His fingers speared into her hair, his thumb brushing her temple. 'What do you want, Cassie?' he asked, his lips slowly descending towards hers.

Cassie was reeling. She could barely think through the fog of pheromones addling her senses, intoxicating her. 'I want you to kiss me,' she whispered, the words flowing thick and heavy like syrup from her throat.

Tuck didn't need it. He swooped the last few centimetres and crushed his mouth against hers. Her lips opened on a whimper that speared straight to his groin, and when her tongue tentatively touched, his heat traced its way there too. He groaned as her mouth opened more and her arms slid around his neck. He pulled her closer, until not even his platinum credit card could have been slipped between them. His hand dropped to her shoulder, skimmed her breast, moulded her hip, and then both his hands moved in unison to the cheeks of her butt hidden beneath layers of fabric.

He pulled her hips in hard, grinding his erection against her. She broke away, gasping, but his lips refused to let her retreat, following and claiming hers again in another hot lashing of lust which she opened to on a tiny little whimper that lit fires in all his erogenous zones.

His hand slid under her shirt, his palm fitting into the small of her back, then moving up the contours of her spine. Up, up, up. Her skin was hot and smooth to touch. The arch of her back, the dip of her ribs, the absence of bra strap fuelled the fever thrumming in his blood. Lust jabbed him in the solar plexus and he jerked her harder against him.

He needed her naked. He needed her laid out on his bed. He needed her calling his name and scratching her nails down his back. He dragged his mouth from hers.

Cassie swayed at the sudden loss of her anchor. The mewing noise coming from somewhere in her throat was totally foreign to her ears. His scent filled her head and drummed against her body like fat drops of sweet, sticky rain.

She couldn't think. All she could do was feel as her senses took over. Taste, touch, hearing, sight, smell.

Dear God, the addictive scent of him.

She blinked up at him. 'Wha...?'

Tuck's groin surged at her bewildered look, at the arousal dilating her pupils with undiluted desire. 'Bed,' he said, his hands sliding down her arms, his fingers linking through hers as he tugged on them gently, pulling her forward as he walked backwards.

The backs of his calves hit the mattress and he stopped. The soft downlights over the bed glowed across her flushed cheeks and glittered in her lust-drunk eyes. Some of her hair had loosened from its ponytail and she looked a little wild. Her ravaged lips and the way they were parted in silent invitation pushed her into wanton territory.

She looked one hundred percent into him and he couldn't remember the last time a woman had looked at him like that—for what he could give her in that moment as opposed to the rest of her life. Not even his ex-wife April had done that. There was no agenda, no artifice. Just a woman who wanted him—Samuel Tucker the man. Not the star quarterback.

Not his money. Not his ring. Not his babies.

Just him.

Frankly, he'd never been more attracted to a woman in his life. He smiled at her as he drew her close, his hands cupping her face again. 'You're very beautiful,' he said.

The words flowed right over Cassie. She didn't care about that. Beauty was superfluous when the attraction was chemical. She didn't need it. She just needed the smell of his skin, the thud of his pulse, the primal act of joining.

He dipped his head and pressed a kiss to her eye, to her cheek, to her temple, his hands dropping by his sides. Cassie turned her face, her cheek brushing the roughness of his. A gust of his earthy male essence fanned over her like a hot dry wind. He kissed down her neck and her nose brushed the angle of his jaw. His aroma intensified. She pushed it against his skin and breathed in long and deep.

Her belly clenched and she groaned out loud. 'You smell so good,' she muttered.

Tuck lifted his head. Her pupils looked even more dilated than before. She was really getting off on those pheromones. He grinned. 'You smell pretty good yourself.' And he dropped his head again to claim her mouth.

But Cassie was suddenly overwhelmed by the urge to smell him. All over. To push her nose into the fat pounding pulse in his throat, to sniff at his temple, to smell his hair. To explore lower—to know the scent of his chest and his belly and his thighs.

To suck in great, big, dizzying lungfuls of him.

She evaded his mouth as it descended, her nose finding the steady beat pulsing along the hard ridge of his throat. It was warm, and his whiskers prickled her skin, smelling sweet yet somehow utterly male. She sucked in big deep breaths, each one washing over her in hot, satisfying waves. But it wasn't enough. She moved up, following the dips of his trachea to the pulse that beat where throat met jaw.

She inhaled deeply there too, dragging in his essence, feeling it lighten her head and tighten her belly. She meandered left along the line of his jaw, breathing him deep into her lungs as she went, and when she reached where the angle of his jaw met his ear she moaned involuntarily as heat bloomed through her pelvis.

Tuck's hands tightened on Cassie's waist as her moan filled his head. His eyes had shut as she'd explored his neck. Her nose and lips buzzing up his throat had sent heat to far-flung areas of his body. He pulled away from her, his heart pounding in his chest, the need to kiss her, to taste her mouth again, too powerful to resist.

For a second they just looked at each other, only the sound of their uneven breath between them. Then her nostrils flared, and her tongue darted out to swipe across her bottom lip, and lust kicked Tuck hard in his gut.

'Cassie,' he muttered, his head swooping down to claim her mouth again.

But Cassie evaded its trajectory, her head filled with one blinding imperative. *His scent.*

'Cassie?'

'I'm sorry,' she said, her chest rising and falling with difficulty, as if every oxygen molecule inside her was drenched in the sticky seduction of his pheromones. 'Can I just...sniff you for a while?'

Tuck laughed, but it died a quick death when he realised she was serious. The woman was definitely getting off on the smell of him. It was such a completely innocent thing to want amidst the carnal lure of lust surrounding them. And God knew it was a lot more satisfying than the women who got off on his fame, or the idea they were going to be the next Mrs Samuel Tucker.

She was looking at him with uncertainty clouding her blue-grey eyes and he wanted the breathy, needy Cassie back. He put his hands up in surrender. Cassie obviously had some kind of itch she wanted to scratch—he was just pleased she'd chosen him to relieve it.

'Whatever floats your boat, darlin'.'

Cassie didn't hesitate. His heady aroma was drawing her back to him with all the power of a magnetic force. She pushed her nose back into his neck, greedily refamiliarising herself with his thick, luscious tang.

'Yes,' she whispered as she moved down this time. 'Yes.'

Tuck swallowed as her breath licked heat down to the hollow at the base of his throat, her moan as she inhaled there fanning his arousal. She lingered for a moment or two, then travelled lower, her nose invading the soft towelling of his robe, moving it sideways as she followed the hard ridge of his collarbone. She reached for the belt of his robe and tugged. When the robe gaped open his erection bucked against the confines of his underwear and he grasped her hips for stability as a wave of red-hot lust almost brought him to his knees.

He hung on silently and waited, his erection aching as she stared at his chest, her nostrils flaring. Then she lifted her hands and pushed the robe off his shoulders. He shrugged them and it fell to the ground, and when she buried her face in the centre of his chest it took all his willpower not to envelop her with his arms, to remember this was *her* show.

After what seemed an age she lifted her head and said, 'Back,' as she pushed on his chest.

Tuck let her push him onto the bed and sat on the mattress looking up at her as she stood between his spread thighs, looking down. Her cheeks were flushed and something base glittered in her eyes.

'All the way,' she muttered, and he obediently fell back against the mattress, his feet still firmly planted on the floor.

He didn't care that he was in nothing but his underwear, with a monster erection threatening to bust free. She was staring at his body with carnal intent and he was totally in her thrall.

'Take your hair down,' he murmured.

Much to his surprise she did it without argument, obviously automatically, with her mind on other things. She was blissfully unaware of how sexy it was, cascading around her shoulders. He smiled at the economy of movement. Other women would have given it a sexy little shake, or piled it up high on their heads and let if drift down as they shimmied about seductively.

But not this one.

Cassie didn't even know where to start as she stared down at him. She was blind to the dips and hollows, the planes and angles, the magnificence of him on anything other than a primal level. How biologically defined he was to hunt and protect. To mate. To procreate. Not even the erection straining his underwear registered on anything other than a scientific level.

She couldn't think past the scent of him—as if it was made specifically for her DNA to recognise and she was the only one who could smell it. Respond to it. His chest pounded with the thump of his heart and his belly bounded to the corresponding pump of his aorta.

Her nostrils flared. *There.* Right there.

She nudged her knee on the bed between his legs and barely registered his sharp intake of breath as she bent over his belly and nuzzled the firm flesh covering the jump of his abdominal pulse. She moaned as her senses filled with him.

And then it wasn't enough. She needed more. She needed to know all of him. She drifted up the centre of his belly, meandering her nose and mouth across his nipples and then drifting further, pushing them into the clean scent of his armpits, feeling the light caress of downy hair against her face. He smelled like soap and deodorant and the scent she was recognising as pure Tuck, and her breasts tingled in response.

She moved up to his throat and jaw again, brushing his temple, rubbing her face in his hair, where something fresh and woodsy flared her nostrils and undulated along her pelvic floor.

Then it was time to head south again. Her nose brushed his, his husky breathing in time with hers, she buzzed his mouth and smelled beer, and felt the rush of air and heat as a low moan slipped from his lips. She went lower, back down his throat, his chest, his belly. It clenched beneath her ministrations and she looked up at him. His eyes were closed, his mouth parted, his fingers clenched in the sheet beside him.

Her chin brushed material as she looked down at the final frontier. She wanted to know what he smelled like *there*. She stood back on her feet and reached for the band of his underwear.

Tuck's eyes flew open as he grabbed her hand. 'Oh, no, you don't,' he said, looking at her through a haze of lust. 'I'm down to my underwear and you're still fully clothed. Time to level the playing field, don't you think?'

Cassie blinked. Tuck's Texan drawl seemed even more pronounced now it was all husky to boot. She looked down at herself. Her state of dress had been the furthest thing from her mind. 'Right,' she said.

Another woman would have felt shy about getting naked before a man for the first time, but Cassie didn't have a problem with it. Hers was just another female body, after all. Just like every other woman's on earth.

Just biology.

She quickly shrugged out of her shirt and shimmied out of her leggings with Tuck watching every move. When his breath hissed out she looked up to find him staring at her, his gaze firmly fixed on her naked breasts.

Her nipples beaded beneath his scrutiny and muscles deep inside her clenched hard.

His gaze drifted lower, to her underwear, and the juncture of her thighs burned and tingled as if he'd blasted her with a hot blue laser beam. She struggled to rein in her choppy breath.

His hoot of laughter was quite unexpected.

'"*Talk nerdy to me*"?' he asked.

Cassie looked down at the logo on her underwear. Again, not something she'd thought about changing. Not that she'd brought anything sexy to change into. Not that she owned anything sexy in the underwear department.

'Let me guess. Gina?'

Cassie shook her head. 'Actually, these are from Reese.'

Tuck laughed again, letting his head fall back against the mattress. Which was all the invitation Cassie needed. He'd wanted a level playing field—he'd got it. Now she wanted her pound of flesh. She looked down at his underwear, her gaze snagging on the erection, and her mouth watered.

She placed one hand on the bed beside him and used the other to reach for the band of his underwear. He sucked in a loud breath and lifted his head off the mattress. Their gazes meshed. They didn't say a word, but he lifted his hips and Cassie stripped his underwear away, pulling it off his feet before coming close again, looking down at him.

Cassie had seen her fair share of penises in her life. She'd known a few intimately. Although none had managed to produce anywhere near the screeching level of arousal that Tuck's had—especially from sight alone! And she'd seen them in all their variation in hundreds of textbooks over the years. She'd never found them particularly attractive, and had pretty much felt that one wasn't that much different from another.

Which just went to show what kind of a freaking genius she was!

Tuck's was the most beautiful specimen she'd ever seen. Long and thick, nestled in light curls, and lying hard and potent against his belly. A fat vein ran up the middle, and once again her mouth watered.

She dropped to her knees without thinking, kneeling between his as she pushed her face against it, running her nose up and down the length of the vein, inhaling its essence. Musk and man.

Tuck's groan, his hand in her hair, his strangled, 'Cassie...' drove her on.

She shifted from the rampant thrust of him to the flat of his belly beneath, and further afield to the heat of his groin, dragging the scent of him inside her as she went. But it was inevitable that she'd return to his erection—as if that was the source of his pheromones, the mother lode—and she inhaled deeply as her lips brushed his girth. She followed it all the way to the head, marvelling at how the skin could feel soft like a rose petal but the core as strong as steel.

A bead of fluid at the tip wafted more musk her way and without conscious thought her tongue dipped into it, savouring its tang as it joined the heady mix intoxicating her senses.

Tuck reared up, cursing. 'Okay—no,' he said, dragging

her up his body and falling back with her, rolling so he pinned her to the bed.

A man could only take so much.

'Enough,' he growled. 'My turn.'

And he flayed her mouth with a kiss full of heat and want and something else he wasn't familiar with and didn't care to know about.

Cassie just held on as his kiss spun her onto another plane. Heat swept through her body and she welcomed it. Yes. *This* was what her body was craving. *This*.

Primitive. Base. Primal.

His hands pushed at her knickers and she helped him, wriggling and kicking until she was free of them, desperate to have him inside her, to quell her hormones for once and for all.

'Yes,' she said against his mouth. 'Now.'

Time to do it. To do what she'd come to do. To get it over with. She'd had her fill of his pheromones. Now it was time for more.

To couple. To mate. To copulate.

Tuck's mind was spinning into a quagmire of lust and desire he could barely find his way out of. He had to slow it down or he was going to explode.

'Slow down, there,' he murmured as he eased a hand between her legs.

Cassie froze. *No!* This wasn't what this was about. It was about exorcising the power of her hormones, satisfying her libido and then moving on. Getting it out of her system. Her hormones had demanded she mate—she was mating.

It was biochemistry. Biology.

It was business. Not pleasure.

Not that pleasure had ever been a possibility for her. And she sure as hell wasn't going to open herself to that dry old argument when she had a paper to get back to.

'No,' she gasped against his mouth, pushing his hand aside as she grabbed his erection. 'I need you in me now.'

She did. She really did. She needed to shut her hormones up for once and all!

'But I want to—'

Cassie cut him off with her mouth, slamming a kiss on his lips that left them dizzy and clinging to each other. *Who knew she could kiss like that?*

'Damn it, Tuck,' she said, breaking away as her hormones screamed at her for fulfilment. '*Now!*'

Tuck was too far gone. Her kiss, and her brand of innocent seduction, and most especially her hand kneading his erection were too, too much—and her whimper when he broke away was a potent aphrodisiac.

'Tuck,' she moaned, grabbing for him.

'Condom,' he said, reaching over the side of the mattress into his bag, locating one in the side zip pocket and quickly donning it.

And then he was back, and Cassie was reaching for him, opening her legs and lifting her hips in invitation, and he took what she was offering, so utterly free of any agenda, and drove himself into her in one easy thrust.

Cassie's gasp was loud in his ears and he stopped abruptly. 'Are you okay?' he asked, looking down at her. Her face was scrunched up.

She wasn't a virgin, was she?

Cassie could feel the hot length of him hard inside her

and doubted she'd ever been filled so completely. It hurt so damn good she swore she could hear her libido sigh.

Yes. *Ahh.* Yes. That was it. *This* was what she needed. 'Yes,' she said.

Yes, yes, yes. It would be over in a minute—two at the outside if Len was any litmus test—and then she'd be free to get on with her life, with her pesky libido back in its box.

She shifted restlessly beneath him. 'Don't stop.'

Tuck obliged, rising up on his elbows, looming over her as he began a slow, teasing thrust guaranteed to satisfy. Arousal streaked hot fingers into his thighs and buttocks as her tightness massaged and squeezed the length of him, and he knew he was going to need all his staying power to hold out for her.

Cassie moaned. She might never have found sex to be personally fulfilling, but she'd always enjoyed the feel of a man inside her and got satisfaction from the pleasure her partner derived from it. As if she'd engineered a successful experiment. And she was determined that today would be no different. Tuck would find his release soon and she could bask in the happy glow of a job well done.

And so, damn it, could her libido.

Of course it was hard to concentrate on the end game when Tuck insisted on such slow, rhythmic thrusts. She didn't like the feeling of pressure building in her pelvis. She'd been there before and knew it never amounted to anything—that it only ever got so far and no more.

Tuck adjusted the angle of his thrust as Cassie lay passively in his arms. He smiled down at the look of concentration on her face. 'Stop thinking,' he growled, leaning in to press a hard kiss on her mouth. It was satisfying to see when he pulled away that he'd kissed the lust back. 'Stop thinking,' he reiterated.

Cassie shut her eyes briefly as he picked up the pace and something stirred deep inside her. Something she didn't like. Something that she knew intuitively she'd never be able to contain.

And that just wasn't part of the world she lived in.

It reminded her too much of a time during her teenage years when her grip on the world had loosened and things had rapidly spiralled out of her control.

A place she never wanted to revisit.

'Don't wait for me,' she dismissed. 'I may take for ever.'

Tuck grinned. 'We've got all night. And I'm not going without you, darlin'.''

Cassie knew with sudden clarity that he was telling the truth, and a surge of dread rose in her chest. For some strange reason she didn't want to appear sexually inadequate before him. But just thinking about the impossibility of it all made her instantly tense.

Tuck groaned, dropping his head to her neck. 'God, you feel so tight,' he muttered, dropping kisses on her throat.

Cassie sighed. There was only one thing for it—and she thanked Gina and Marnie and Reese for making her watch that movie where the actress faked an orgasm in a coffee shop, because at least she had some clue how to go about it.

She shut her eyes and started to moan, softly at first, then picking up, adding in some panting—and didn't she remember seeing another film with the Awesome Foursome where the actress dug her nails into the actor's back a lot, even scratched them down? She threw that in for good measure.

Tuck felt the bite of Cassie's nails right down to his groin, and cried out as her moans and pants pushed him closer to the edge. He picked up the pace, dropping his forehead against hers as their orgasms built and built. Cassie's cries got louder, and when she reached for his buttocks and squeezed tight his orgasm hit warp speed.

'Yes, Tuck, yes,' Cassie croaked in his ear, knowing he was close and gasping her pleasure, no matter how fake, right into his ear.

She was too busy concentrating on faking it to be in tune with the buzz going on inside her, but that was okay. If Tuck's big hard body pounding into hers hadn't satisfied her libido than nothing would.

'Tuck,' she cried. 'Tuck. I'm... I'm...'

Tuck's belly pulled taut and red-hot pleasure eddied and swirled just out of his reach as his orgasm bubbled to the surface. 'Yes, Cassie, yes. Let go. I'll come with you.'

Cassie cried out in what she hoped was a fairly accurate rendition of an orgasming woman. It certainly seemed to convince Tuck, who groaned her name as he thrust and thrust and thrust, causing a little more tension to gather in her pelvis.

Cassie let her cries die down in pace with his as he collapsed on top of her. She might not have been satisfied in the strictest sense of the word, but there was something very primitive and sating about being possessed so utterly.

Something carnal. Hormonal.

Tuck stirred, kissing Cassie's neck, her collarbone. He rolled off her onto his back with a long contented groan, his heart still pounding like a train, his head spinning from one of the most forceful orgasms he'd ever had. For long moments he couldn't even move.

When he was capable of stirring he rolled up onto his elbow and looked down into her face, needing to know that it had been as good for her. To see that look he knew so well. That *Paper? What paper?* look.

Instead she smiled at him and patted his biceps. 'That was nice,' she chirped.

Nice? Tuck eyed her suspiciously. There were three things he was good at in life—football, math and sex.

And there was nothing *nice* about his brand of sex.

He'd slept with a lot of women—which wasn't necessarily something to be proud of, but he knew for a damn fact not one of them had left his bed anything other than one hundred percent satisfied. He was satisfaction *guaranteed.* And as such he knew the signs. Could read it in their eyes.

Hell, he could pick a sated woman out of a line-up at fifty paces.

He would not have picked Cassie out of a line-up.

'Oh, my God,' he murmured. 'You faked it.'

FIVE

———

TUCK FLOPPED ON to his back. No one had ever—*ever*—faked it with him. That wasn't arrogance or conceit—it was the damn plain truth of it.

It was ironic that he'd just had one of those *oh-my-god* moments and she was lying there all *that-was-nice*. He stared at the ceiling, trying to decide whether he should be insulted, but he found himself laughing instead.

Somehow it seemed par for the course for this very bizarre seduction.

Cassie felt his low laughter stroke deep inside her to muscles and tissues that still seemed tense and excitable. She frowned. They weren't supposed to be like that—they were supposed to be loose, limber.

Done. Content. Over.

Gina's warning that once might not be enough came back to haunt her. *Well, too bad!* She'd given in to the insanity of her libido and now she wanted her brain back!

Tuck shook his head, still contemplating the ceiling. 'I can't believe you faked it.' And he laughed again.

'Look, it's okay,' Cassie assured him, eyes also firmly

trained on the ceiling as she went into the familiar patter. Len had required a lot of reassurance in the beginning too. 'It's not your fault. It's me... I'm just not
physically capable of climaxing. It has nothing to do
with your technique...or your speed—'

Tuck laughed harder, interrupting her clueless cri-
tique. He rolled up on his elbow again. 'Darlin', you are
hard on a man's ego.'

Cassie blinked and her nostrils flared as a heady dose
of pheromones engulfed her. Those muscles inside her
snapped to attention, pulling taut and sizzling with tension.

No. *No, no, no.*

Concentrate. Soothe the man's ego and then take your
libido far, far away. Take it to Cornell and bury it in a
PhD.

'Sorry, I didn't mean... Look, it just doesn't happen
for me. It's a...a thing.'

Tuck saw her pupils dilating again. *Interesting.* 'Like
a medical condition?' he asked innocently as he nuzzled her ear.

Cassie swallowed, her eyelids fluttering closed. 'Kind
of.'

He dropped a kiss on her temple. 'Sounds awful,' he
murmured.

'Oh, no, it's fine,' Cassie said, shaking her head, trying to clear the fog filling it as his scent wrapped her up
in seductive thread. 'I don't need it.'

Tuck smiled against her hair line. If anyone needed an
orgasm it was Cassiopeia. 'Honey,' he said as his mouth

zeroed in on hers, '*everyone* needs a little bit of *it* some-times.'

Cassie opened her eyes to deny his statement just as his mouth made contact with hers, and a wave of longing for *it* crashed over her. It was impossible. How could she crave something she'd never had? Miss something she didn't know? Want something she didn't need?

Where was the logic in that?

But his kiss laid her bare, plundering her mouth, flay-ing her with heat and pheromones, demanding that she kiss him back with equal vigour. And she did—clinging to him, twisting her arms around his neck, attacking his mouth with a savagery utterly foreign to her.

A sense of falling gripped her when he finally pulled away, and Cassie was grateful for being horizontal and anchored to him.

Tuck looked down into her flushed face. She was breathing hard. They both were. They were going again—and this time she was coming with him.

He pulled away. 'I'll be back in a moment,' he said.

Cassie watched him climb out of the bed in a stu-por, her head spinning from the kiss and the dizzying essence of him spinning her in its web. She struggled against it, her brain urging her to be sensible.

She levered herself on her elbows. 'I should go.'

'Oh, no, you don't,' Tuck said as he strode towards the bathroom to rid himself of the condom. 'I haven't fin-ished with you yet.'

Go! her brain screamed. *Go now!*

Her brain willed her muscles to move. But her muscles said no. Every cell in her body, drenched in sex, leadened by his command to stay, said no. And then he was back, striding towards her, gloriously naked, stopping to snag some foil packets from his bag and throwing them on the bedside table. And then he was pushing her back, stroking his hands down her body, finger-painting his pheromones all over her. Stupid took over.

Okay, she accepted as she welcomed the heat of his mouth on hers. *Slight change of plan.* They were going again. She could do that. Obviously another coupling was what her body was craving. She could do it. She could go twice.

And then get back to her paper.

Tuck had no idea what Cassie was thinking as his mouth left hers for parts further south. He was too caught up in being so rampantly hard again, considering what had happened not even ten minutes ago, and he was determined not to waste it. This time it would be about her. No taking.

No faking.

He'd followed the same game plan he always followed when he was with a woman, but had let Cassie's wild urgings and amazing aptitude for acting distract him from his goal. She was going to be singing the *Hallelujah Chorus* tonight if it killed him.

Cassie's head spun and she shut her eyes as Tuck's hot tongue traced a pathway down her throat. What was he *doing*? She was ready. *He* was most definitely ready. Why wasn't he inside her already? She shifted restlessly against him, spreading her legs to accommodate him, lifting her hips.

Tuck smiled, ignoring her blatant invitation. No

way—not this time. He ran his tongue up and over the swell of a breast, and when he reached the nipple he swiped his tongue over it, then sucked it inside, smiling as it leapt to attention in his mouth.

Cassie's eyes flew open as a jolt of sensation pinged along muscle fibres and nerve-endings already at snapping point. Her nipples were extraordinarily sensitive, and having them fondled during sex had always been irritating. She tried to sit up, to tell him to stop, that it wasn't necessary, but his mouth closed over her other nipple and she fell back against the mattress on a whimper.

Tuck was obviously determined to go where no man had ever been—the O zone.

'You know,' she panted, her eyes shut, her back arching off the bed as his teeth grazed and taunted her nipple—which strangely didn't feel irritating at all when he did it. 'You really don't have to do this. To try. I won't think any less of you.'

Tuck ignored her. 'Is that so?' He sucked on her nipple hard, satisfied to hear a strange gurgly noise at the back of her throat.

Cassie resolutely held on to her sanity—no matter how tenuous it suddenly appeared. 'It's really not going to happen, so you might as well just...' she swallowed as his tongue flicked back and forth over the taut peak he was toying with '...get down to business.'

Tuck withdrew his mouth and looked up at her. He could see the moist, puckered stance of her nipple in his peripheral vision, and it was deeply satisfying to know that she was viewing him through the evidence of her own arousal.

'Wanna bet?' He smiled, then returned his attention to the nipple, hungry for the satisfying hardness of it against his palate.

Cassie shut her eyes. 'Is not about chance,' she said, her breath choppy. 'It's statistics. You must understand that, right?' She raised her head to look at him and was hit by a surge of lust at the sight of his blond head bowed over her breast. She flopped back down, pushing it ruthlessly away.

Where was she again?

'I know I'm statistically unlikely to achieve orgasm simply because I never have.'

'Uh-huh,' Tuck said, her nipple slipping from his mouth as he left for more southern destinations.

His hand followed, brushing light strokes down her rib-cage to her hip, across the flat of her belly and fluttering down her thighs. His mouth found her belly button and he lapped wet circles around it, dipping in and out as he went.

Cassie felt every muscle fibre beneath shudder in anticipation. She'd never felt this much tension in her belly before. It was heavy—screeching with it.

'It's not you.' She pressed on, for her sanity's sake if nothing else, as he caressed her inner thigh and she felt it all the way to her centre. 'I take this medication. It helps me sleep. But it...' She panted as his tongue moved lower. 'It suppresses certain other...' A strangled gasp rose in her throat as she felt a finger brush over the place where everything felt slick and wet and tingly. She gulped for air. 'Other processes...'

Tuck raised his head to look at her. He could smell her arousal, and his erection kicked at the thought of tasting her.

He made sure their gazes were locked when he said, 'It just means I have to work a little harder.' He slipped a finger inside her. Her swift intake of breath and the way her hands bunched in the sheet punched him hard in the gut. 'I'm not afraid of hard work.'

Cassie couldn't look away from the compelling determination in his star blue eyes. There were things inside them that she didn't understand—and didn't want to either. She shut her eyes, blocked him out. Blocked out the heaviness in her breasts, the tension in her belly, the hard probe of his finger buried inside her.

'Yes, but how good can it really—?' Another finger slid inside her and she gasped at its intrusion. It took a few moments for her to lamely add, 'Be?'

Sensation swamped her, momentarily drowning out the yammering of her brain before she clawed it back.

'I've seen comet trails,' she panted as he pulled his fingers out and pushed them in again. 'And exploding stars.' More pushing and pulling and panting. 'The birth of universes. Nothing can beat that.'

Tuck looked up from her belly, where he was doodling wet circles with his tongue, withdrawing his fingers. 'Oh, honey, just you lie back,' he murmured. 'Let me teach you some things they don't rate at Mensa.'

And he settled between her legs, pushing them wide with his shoulders, feasting his eyes on the end game.

Her arousal wafted towards him and he salivated at the thought of tasting her. A surge of red-hot lust enveloped him at seeing the thatch of dark hair reminding him she was all woman.

Cassie's eyes widened as Tuck lowered his head and his intent became clear. 'Oh, no,' she said, placing her hand over herself, barring his way. 'No, no, *no*. You definitely don't have to do *that*.'

Tuck looked up. From this vantage point he could see her still erect nipples, standing proud and puckered, and smell her musky scent. He flared his nostrils. It filled his head and it took all his willpower not to bury his face in her. 'I know. But I want to.'

Cassie shook her head. 'Nothing works,' she reiterated. Why wasn't he listening to her?

Tuck's hands slid up her body to stroke her breasts, his fingers smoothing over the taut peaks of her nipples. 'Trust me,' he murmured.

Cassie gasped as his touch bloomed and tingled at the juncture of her thighs, just below where his face hovered. It burned and ached. 'I've never...'

'It's okay.' He grinned. 'I'm an expert.'

And then he lowered his head, nudging her hand aside, just nuzzling her at first, brushing his closed mouth along her sex, familiarising himself with the contours, filling his senses up with her.

Then he let his tongue do some exploring. He swiped it against the centre of her and grunted in satisfaction when she gasped and bucked against him. He inhaled then, deep and long, and his head roared with a surge of lust and male possession and he opened his mouth over her, needing more, wanting all of her.

Cassie felt a jolt of something hot and hard slam into her belly and she shut her eyes against the urgency of it. Tuck's tongue licked and probed and sucked as his fingers spread their own joy, stroking and teasing and rubbing her nipples to a state of almost painful arousal, and she gasped and squirmed beneath the relentless attack.

She lifted her head to look at him, and the sight of his blond head between her legs flushed like a drug through her system. When his tongue found the hard nub that she'd never really bothered to explore for herself and flicked it she just about lifted off the bed.

'Tuck!' she cried out as sensations she'd never experienced before catapulted her into a whole new realm.

Tuck's hand moved down from her breast to splay low and wide on her belly, clamping her to the mattress, holding her earthbound as she bucked and writhed beneath the onslaught of his tongue. He was holding her right where she was, taunting her with all he had, tasting her, determined to make her so rattled she wouldn't know which solar system she was in.

And all the time a primal beat thrummed through his head and streaked hot urgency through the muscles of his belly and buttocks. He was torn between the overriding urge to drive into her, to plunge himself into all that tight heat and feel her around him again, and the need to suck up every last morsel of her, to feast on her, to propel her to a place she'd never been.

A place more cosmic than she'd ever seen.

Cassie didn't know what was happening to her as heat

and pressure built everywhere, but she was suddenly terrified. She hadn't felt anything like this before but she knew with a disturbing clarity that she wanted it—bad.

And that was the most frightening thing of all.

The only thing she'd ever wanted this badly was to go to Antarctica on a research mission, and now even that seemed to pale in comparison to the tidal force of lust and seething need consuming her body.

Her life dealt in certainties. Fact and logic and common sense were her true north. She depended on them. She needed them. And this...whatever it was...was making a mockery of them.

If this was the power of an orgasm she could do without.

'No,' she muttered, her head tossing from side to side, her eyes shut fast. She didn't want this. 'No.'

'Yes,' Tuck said, sensing that most of the battle was inside Cassie's head. He held her fast and sucked down hard on her clitoris. 'Stop fighting it, Cassie,' he said when he finally lifted his head.

Cassie shook her head. 'No,' she muttered as sensations rose and she pushed them back.

Tuck grimaced. He knew she was there, that she was on the edge, so close. *Goddamn it,* he'd never met a woman so averse to a good time in his life.

'Yes,' he said, shifting his hand off her belly and using it in tandem with his tongue, stroking his index finger up and down her centre as his other hand ministered to the tight pucker of her nipples.

She didn't need to have this in her life—to change

everything she'd thought she knew. She knew what she wanted. And it wasn't the total consuming vortex of sex.

Tuck urged her on, pushing a finger inside all her tight, slick heat. And then another.

Cassie gaped at the invasion. Something started to pool and ripple, down low and deep, and hot urgent fingers dug into her buttocks and thighs. But she clamped down hard against it, pushing it back. Her heels drummed against the mattress. Her head rocked from side to side.

Tuck looked up at her. Her head was thrown back, her mouth open, gasping with every thrust of his fingers. 'I can show you some stars, darlin', like you've never seen before,' he murmured. 'You just gotta let go.'

Cassie whimpered. *Let go?* What did that mean? She didn't know *how* to let go.

'Relax, let it take you,' Tuck soothed as she cried out in obvious conflict.

Cassie sobbed as the effort to push back the looming tide threatened to overwhelm her. Nothing was familiar. Nothing was the same. Everything was coming apart around her as a swirling, sucking sensation deep in her core obliterated all thought and consciousness and finally pulled her into its abyss.

Tuck felt her clamp tight around his fingers and knew she was finally there. He dropped his head and lashed his tongue back and forward over the nub that had grown impossibly hard. Her back arched off the bed and he squeezed her nipple between his fingers.

Cassie cried out as her mind left her body and flew. Tuck had promised her stars, and as deep, unremitting pleasure drenched her she floated through a cosmos of colours, with a kaleidoscope of shooting stars bursting around her like fireworks. She was actually amongst them—not just observing them from afar. Reaching out for them. Basking in their heat and absorbing their incandescence into her soul.

Tuck did not let up, feasting greedily until Cassie's muscles stopped contracting around him and the cries and the wild bucking of her hips started to settle. He gently withdrew his fingers from her, propping his chin on her belly as he watched them die to a hush, waiting for the moment that she opened her eyes.

And he wasn't disappointed. When she finally lay spent and still on the mattress, and her eyes eventually fluttered open, the blue-grey was practically slate with drunken satisfaction, her pupils big and black, her focus obviously not quite twenty-twenty as she blinked at him rapidly.

'Tuck?'

Now he could pick her out of a line-up.

Now she didn't even look as if she could *spell* the word *paper*.

'I... I...'

Tuck smiled at her utter bewilderment, but it grabbed a big handful of his gut and squeezed hard. He grinned, crawling up her body, dropping a kiss on her belly, and one between her breasts and the hollow at the base of her throat, before lashing her mouth with a deep, wet kiss, his erection surging as it pressed into her thigh.

'Hold on, darlin',' he muttered against her mouth as he reached for a foil packet, 'we're not done yet.'

Cassie watched, still in a daze, as he tore at the packet with his teeth. There weren't a lot of coherent thoughts in her head, but her stomach clenched at the sight of him, hard and ready, and once again her brain went on vacation as her body responded to the primal cue to mate.

And then he was over her, and in her, his mouth drugging her with kisses that took her back to that place amongst the stars, and his erection was stroking inside her, reviving tissues that were already in a dangerously excitable state. And she was flying again, but it was better this time because he was with her, and she held on to him tight as they astral-planed through the cosmos, revelling in the shake and the shudder of him, his guttural cries in her ear ratcheting the pleasure up, taking her higher and higher and higher.

Cassie didn't know how long they were gone for. Or how long it took to come back down to earth. Time ceased to exist and the awareness of her surroundings crept back very slowly. The mattress beneath her. The weight of his body on hers. The sound of their breath as they lay together, gasping.

All these years and *that* was what she'd been missing out on?

At some stage Tuck rolled off her, getting up to dispose of the condom, then rejoined her, lying down next to her as she stared at the ceiling, contemplating the magic that had just happened.

When she finally got her breath back she said, 'Please tell me you can do that again.'

Obviously her brain was still missing in action.

Tuck rolled his head to look at her and laughed. It looked as if one round of good sex had turned Little-Miss-Brainiac into Little-Miss-Nymphomaniac. 'I may need a moment or two.'

Cassie was pretty sure she was going to need some recovery time too. She turned on her side, her gaze roving over his face. 'Is it...is it always like that?'

Tuck nodded, but he knew that wasn't true. What they'd just had wasn't like anything else he'd ever experienced. Sex had always been good, but never like this. Not even with April, whom he'd thought he'd loved. Or tried to anyway.

The knowledge was unsettling.

He rolled his head back to stare at the ceiling again. 'It is with me, darlin',' he said, keeping up his usual patter.

Cassie got goose bumps as the low, slow drawl of Tuck's accent whispered across her skin and stroked those muscles inside her that didn't seem to be able to get enough of him. Her gaze was drawn to the rise and fall of his chest and she actually reached out and trailed her fingers down it—something, prior to yesterday, she would have thought she'd need a frontal lobotomy to do.

Her cheek rested on his biceps and his scent tickled her senses again. She pressed her nose into the warm bulk and inhaled him deep inside her body. A blast of his natural essence invaded her cells again and stirred the embers of her orgasm.

Tuck smiled. 'I could bottle some of those pheromones, if you like?'

Cassie dragged herself away. Why bottle it when it

was right here? In the flesh? Gina *was* right. Maybe she needed a little time? Like a whole night?

She was leaving in the morning—hopefully with her brain returned—why deprive herself?

'Direct from the source is always best,' she said, trying to sound scientific and factual when she felt tongue-tied and unsure of herself.

Tuck grinned as he looked down at her. 'Don't you have a paper to get back to?'

Cassie nodded. She did. She really did. But she was pretty sure even simple words were beyond her at the moment, let alone complex analysis of weather patterns on Jupiter. Not to mention the fact that for the first time in her life she actually didn't *care* about the complex weather systems of Jupiter.

'I'm not sure I'll understand it. I think I just lost a hundred IQ points.'

Tuck chuckled. 'Welcome to being average. I hope you enjoy your stay.'

If this was how average people passed their time Cassie was beginning to think that being a genius was the dumbest thing anyone could be.

'I'm leaving for Cornell in the morning,' she said. She had no idea where it had come from, but there was obviously still one functioning brain cell somewhere that seemed to remember what had been *the most important thing in her life* until half an hour ago.

Tuck rolled up in one swift movement, settling himself into the cradle of her hips. 'So tonight we'll just play dumb. How's it been so far?'

Cassie blinked. 'Very...educational.'

'Oh, so you approve of my copulation techniques?' he teased. 'Your libido has been adequately serviced?'

Cassie might have been clueless about a lot of things but, having read a lot of textbooks and seen a lot of nature shows, even *she* was aware that what they'd just shared was nothing to do with the slaking of a biological imperative.

'Well, I have minimal comparative data, and no blind studies to—'

Tuck's mouth cut her off and she lost her mind for a while as his scent filled her up with heady need. When he pulled back they were both a little out of breath.

'I'll take that as a no,' he said. 'It's okay. I'll try harder. They don't call me Mr-Satisfaction-Guaranteed for nothing. Libido servicing is right up my alley. Are you hungry?'

'It's almost midnight,' she murmured. Cassie never ate after seven o'clock. It wasn't good for the digestion.

Tuck shrugged. 'So?'

Cassie blinked as a huge belly rumble echoed in the space between them and she realised she was starving. She'd become a truly primitive woman—utterly biological. 'I could go for some toast.'

Tuck smiled as he dropped a hard kiss on her mouth and reached over and snatched up the phone. 'Trust me—you'll like what I can do with strawberries and cream much better.'

Cassie woke wrapped spoon-like in Tuck's arms at eight the next morning. It was the second morning in a row she'd woken late. The second morning in a row she'd woken thinking about him. The second morning in a row she'd woken with Jupiter as far from her brain as the actual planet itself.

And the first morning ever she'd woken with a man rubbing all his rampant male hardness against her. Tuck's hand was at her breast, and his essence filled her waking senses with sex and surrender, giving her brain no chance to switch on.

Tuck sensed the moment she came awake and his hand tightened around the swell of her breast, his fingers rolling over her nipple. When she moaned and arched her back he dragged her closer, kissing her neck.

'When do you have to leave?' he muttered in her ear.

Leave? Cassie thought hard through the fog of pheromones and the heavy scent of sex clouding her senses. 'Whenever I can get a train,' she said.

Tuck licked a path from her ear to the slope where her shoulder met her throat as his hand slipped between her legs. 'When do you *need* to be at Cornell?'

Cassie shut her eyes as his fingers stroked against her centre. 'Day...after...tomorrow...' she murmured, easing her legs apart to give him better access.

'So you could stay another night?' he said, his finger sinking into the slick heat of her. 'Just to make sure your libido is well and truly serviced. I'd hate for that to get in the way of your very important studies.'

Cassie thought he made a very good point—just as he found the spot that was screaming for his touch. She gasped. 'Yes. That would be awful. I need to focus at Cornell.' She needed her libido back in its box. 'I could do one more night.'

Tuck was too far gone to acknowledge his triumph. All he could feel was the wet heat of her as he slid his erection up and down the length of her slick entrance—close, so close.

'Do you have any condoms in your room?' he asked.

Cassie squirmed against him, tilting her pelvis, desperately needing him inside her, not taunting her from the outside. 'Why would *I* have condoms?'

Tuck groaned, trying to wrestle back control. 'We're out.' And a place as posh as the Bellington wasn't likely to have a condom vending machine. '*Somebody* was insatiable last night.'

Cassie blushed. She'd lost count of the number of orgasms she'd had. They'd all just blurred together into one long brain-incapacitating event.

Tuck pulled away from her with difficulty. Even knowing he couldn't get any woman pregnant, he'd always been a stickler for safe sex. He reached for the telephone. 'I'll ring the concierge.'

Cassie dragged in gulps of air, trying to clear the sexual fog, but as per usual all she did was drag in more of him and her belly tightened. She rolled onto her back, her head turning towards him. 'The concierge will get you condoms?'

'The concierge will get a star quarterback whatever the hell he likes.'

'Even an *ex*?' she asked, trying to imagine a famous astronomer—*real* stars, in her opinion—getting the same treatment.

Tuck flinched slightly at the *ex*. For well over a decade he'd defined himself by the magic he'd made on the field. It still cut deep that it had all been snatched away. But he pushed it aside. 'Yup.'

Cassie tried to fathom the celebrity paradigm, but even that was too much with her brain gone walkabout. 'Wait,' she said as he went to dial. 'I'll ring Gina.'

Tuck frowned. 'Why not the concierge?'

'Because Gina already knows we're doing it.'

And the fewer people who knew she'd lost her mind the better.

SIX

CASSIE AND TUCK stayed another *two* nights. Just to be sure her libido was well and truly serviced. They rose late on the third morning, had a dirty shower and, unable to avoid the phone calls and text messages from her gal pals any longer, Cassie joined them in the dining room for a late breakfast.

'Well, well, well,' Gina drawled as Cassie sat down. 'Never thought I'd see the day. Cassiopeia Barclay all loved up.'

Cassie snorted. 'Don't be ridiculous. Love is a romantic construct—'

'Perpetrated by romance novels and Hollywood with no sound scientific basis,' Gina finished.

Cassie shot her a sheepish look. 'Exactly.' She fiddled with her cutlery. 'Tuck and I are just—'

'Copulating?' Reese said, winking at Gina.

Cassie nodded, even though she knew they'd moved far beyond copulation. Beyond scratching a biological itch. Her libido had been well and truly satisfied after the first twenty-four hours—it was just being plain greedy now. 'Yes.'

'And has Tuck copulated his way through my box of condoms yet?' Gina asked.

Cassie almost said he'd copulated her brains out as she thought about how many of those condoms they had used. Their wet, slippery shower sex this morning stirred her olfactory centre and she blushed under the scrutiny of three sets of eyes. She'd blushed more in the last three days than she had her entire life.

Three things she didn't do was blush, swoon or cry, and she was two out of three at the moment. It was just as well she was leaving today and could get back to being someone she recognised.

'Not quite,' she said.

'I can't believe you and Tuck...' Reese shook her head. 'I thought for sure he was bound to date blonde airheads for the rest of his life.'

'April wasn't blonde,' Marnie said. 'Or an airhead. She was a nurse, wasn't she?'

Reese nodded. 'They met while he was having his knee reconstruction. She was nice...sweet. But they were married for less than *two years*. And now he's back to dating surgically enhanced pneumatic blondes again.'

'Except for Cassie,' Gina mused, and all three women looked at her again, sitting at the dining table in a baggy T-shirt proclaiming *'Geek is the new sexy'*, her long straight dark brown hair scraped back in a low ponytail and Alice band, her messy eyebrows knitted together.

'We're not dating,' Cassie reiterated. 'We're—'

'Copulating,' her friends said in unison, then laughed.

Cassie smiled at their infectious happiness. 'Well, we're not even doing that any more. I'm leaving today, and nothing is more important to me now than finishing my PhD and being on that plane to Antarctica next year.'

'Good for you,' Marnie said.

'Make sure you talk to me before you go. A designer friend of mine is making a huge splash in sexy thermal-wear,' Gina said, raising her coffee cup.

Cassie blinked. 'I think they issue us with thermals.'

Gina shuddered. 'I can just imagine what *they'd* be like.'

Reese laughed at the blank look on Cassie's face. 'How are you getting to Cornell?'

'Tuck's giving me a lift to New York and I'll get a bus to Ithica from there.'

Reese raised an eyebrow. Mr Love-'em-and-Leave-'em, who'd told her a few days ago he was staying on at the Hamptons at a friend's place for a week, was dropping his plans and heading back to New York?

Interesting. Very interesting...

In the end Tuck insisted on driving her all the way to Cornell in his big black BMW. She'd protested about the distance, but he'd just shrugged and said he enjoyed a road trip. It took five hours from the Hamptons, and there wasn't one minute of it when Cassie wasn't aware of the length and breadth of him, of his heat, of his scent.

The aroma she'd come to recognise as pure Tuck—*to respond to like Pavlov's dog*—filled the inside of the cab, completely obliterating the luxury car smell and enveloping her in a hormonal fugue all the way to Ithica. She vaguely remembered them talking about her study and about his app, but the details were fuzzy.

It was late afternoon when they arrived—not that the long summer day gave any indication of the hour. The campus was surprisingly bustling for the mid-year break. Young people were laughing and smiling in groups, carrying books and laptops, or sitting on the grass under shady trees, engrossed in their phones or other electronic gadgets.

It took them an hour to locate her accommodation block and check in. Tuck helped her up with her bags. The corridors were buzzing with what Tuck soon found out to be high school students when he was recognised. He stopped for a chat and posed for pictures while he signed autographs for some very excited kids.

Cassie watched on, bemused, as Tuck high-fived and talked about football and retirement and his knee. The students—from Wisconsin—were doing Summer College, studying entomology, and he talked to them about the importance of getting an education. They buzzed around him like the insects they were studying, and she began to wonder if everything with a pulse was attracted to his seriously addictive pheromones.

Eventually they let him leave and she found her room, unlocking the door and pushing it open. Tuck carried her bag through. 'I can't believe,' he said as he set her suitcase on the single bed, 'you've come here for three months *from Australia* and that's all you brought. Most women I know take a suitcase that size away for the weekend. For their make-up.'

She shrugged as she looked round the small but functional room. 'I don't care much for clothes.'

Tuck looked her up and down and chuckled at the understatement. He'd always appreciated women's packaging, but after three days in bed with Cassie he was never judging a book by its cover again.

'I agree,' he said as he thought about all the delight hidden beneath her voluminous shirts and how long it had been since he'd seen it. The shower seemed a very long time ago. 'I think they're highly overrated.'

Cassie felt the drop in his voice's pitch undulate through the muscles deep inside her that had already received such an athletic workout back in the Hamptons. She glanced at him. He had his hands shoved in the pockets of the trendy three-quarter chinos he wore with a polo shirt sporting some kind of NFL logo, and a surge of pheromones hit her square between the eyes.

She looked away, her glance falling on the only horizontal surface in the room—the bed. She looked back at him. She'd spent practically every waking and sleeping hour of the last three days in bed with the man looking at her now as if he was calculating how quickly he could get her out of her clothes.

A shout in the corridor, followed by some heavy footsteps, yanked her back from the ledge.

Tuck dragged his eyes off Cassie, raking his hand through his hair. Unfortunately they found the bed. The narrow single bed—staple of the college dorm all over the country. He'd spent a lot of his college life on a bed just like it. Or beds just like it, anyway. And he knew from experience they weren't made for long, lazy sessions with a woman.

They were made for haste, not finesse, and paper-thin walls didn't guarantee ambience *or* privacy. At eighteen that hadn't been an issue, but at thirty-three, with a bad knee and various other aches and pains, he was way too old to fold himself into a bed not fit for an athlete.

No matter how tempting it was to yank her into his arms and go hunting for that body he knew was under all those layers. He looked around the tiny room and thanked God he never had to live like this again.

'Why are you here? Doesn't a place as esteemed as Cornell have some better digs for its PhD students?'

Cassie nodded. 'Sure. But this is cheap—which is important when you've been a professional uni student for over a decade. These dorms become vacant over the summer break, so they're keen to fill them and the price is right.'

Tuck's gaze drifted back to the bed as he absorbed her words. It had been a long time since he'd had to give any thought to the cost of living. He had more than enough money from his decade-long career, and enough continuing endorsements never to have to worry about money again. And the app project promised to be another winner.

There was more yahooing in the corridor, and Tuck turned slightly in the direction of a *thunk* as someone obviously hit the wall. A burst of laughter sounded and he turned back to face her. 'Won't that interfere with your study?'

'No. I'll be spending most of my time at the Space

Sciences Building or the observatory,' she said. 'It's just a place to sleep.'

Tuck's gaze was once again drawn to the bed at her mention of sleep. A vision of her on it, with him, most definitely *not* sleeping, filled his head. His groin tightened and he looked at her, the same time she looked at him, and the room seemed to shrink even further.

'It's not a very big bed,' he murmured.

Cassie shrugged. 'There's just me.'

Tuck felt the sudden urge to puff his chest and say something macho like, *Damn straight, there'll just be you!* But then that conjured thoughts of her on this bed by herself, maybe naked, maybe touching herself while she thought about him. *Not that she probably did that.* But the thought stirred the tightening in his groin to a full-blown erection.

His gaze dropped to her mouth and he took a step towards her. Noticed the flare of her nostrils, the dilation of her pupils, her chest rising and falling with the same agitated rhythm as the night of their first kiss.

Cassie shut her eyes briefly as her body swayed towards the chemical cloud she seemed programmed to obey. And she almost took a step too. But the shrill ring of a phone pierced the sound and yanked her back from his hypnotic pull.

She looked around, hindered for a moment by sluggish brain cells and the unfamiliar ring—it wasn't her mobile and nor was it Tuck's.

'Your desk,' Tuck said, stepping back.

Cassie looked at the desk, pushed into a nook not far from the foot of the bed. She identified a slimline black telephone and took the three paces required to snatch it up, grateful for a little distance from Tuck. It was Professor Judy Walsh, who would be working with her on the completion of her PhD, welcoming her to the campus and checking she was good to go in the morning. They had a brief conversation, which Cassie barely took in, conscious as she was of Tuck prowling back and forth behind her like a caged animal.

Every *cell* in her body, every *hair* covering her body vibrated with his physical presence.

When she hung up she was angry. With Tuck. But mostly with herself. Studying at Cornell, the university that had nurtured the genius of greats like Carl Sagan, had been a lifelong dream and she was letting some weird aberration derail her pursuit of her goals.

It was a good thing that Professor Walsh had rung when she had. Exactly what Cassie had needed to refocus. Because the way things had been heading prior to the interruption had precious little to do with astronomy.

Focus, Cassiopeia.

She turned to face Tuck, staying right where she was. The room was small, so distance wasn't an option, but she'd take whatever space she could get. 'Thanks for the lift,' she said. 'But if you don't mind I really have to get settled in. Set up my computer, unpack. Etcetera.'

Tuck regarded her for a moment. Considering the size of her suitcase, and the fact she owned a laptop, he doubted it would take her ten minutes to do all of it. So there was only one conclusion to draw.

She was blowing him off.

He was so stunned for a moment he didn't say anything. Then he threw back his head and laughed. First
she faked it and now she was blowing him off. Two
things *no* woman had ever done to him. She wasn't just
hell on a man's ego—she was death to it.

He had thought of taking her out for a bite to eat, but
she'd obviously scratched her itch and was ready to move
on. No long drawn-out goodbye, no clinging to him and
begging him to call from Little Miss Mensa.

'So this is goodbye, huh?'

Cassie nodded. 'Yes.'

She often felt socially awkward, but this was a whole
other level. She'd never been in the position of having
to bid farewell to a man who had spent a fair portion of
three days camped out between her legs. What did one
say in such circumstances?

'Thank you for...'

For what? For the orgasms? For the copulation? For
the pheromones? For an experiment she'd never forget
as long as she lived?

'Everything,' she ended lamely.

Tuck grinned as he easily read every thought that
flitted through her mind. 'Don't ever play poker, Cassiopeia,' he murmured.

He reached into his pocket for his wallet and pulled
out a card. His real card, with his real phone number—
not the one he gave to hard-to-shake groupies. 'You could
always call me if your libido starts getting a little antsy
again.'

He held it out and she looked at it as if it was a vial
of poison. His grin broadened. Most women in this sit-

uation would have begged him for it. Hell, having his phone number in their hot little hands would probably be a story they'd tell to the end of their days.

Cassie stood her ground by the desk. 'It won't. My brain is firmly back in charge. And there's no room for... that.'

Tuck raised an eyebrow at the finality in her words. He had no doubt she meant it in all those higher functioning areas, of which she had many. She didn't strike him as a woman who let anything ruin her focus—especially now her libido was in check. But it was that little hesitation coming from somewhere deeper that gave him pause.

He strode the three paces that separated them and placed his card on her desk. 'Goodbye, Cassiopeia. It was fun.'

He didn't wait for a response, just turned and walked out through the door. It wasn't until he reached his car that Tuck realised it *had* been fun.

Not fun in the yee-ha, laugh-out-loud, usual way. It hadn't been gambling in Vegas with a pocketful of green and a blonde on his arm, or partying in Paris, or hearing the roar of the crowd coming out at him from under the Thursday night lights. Those had been the things that had defined fun for him until now—especially since his career slump and his marriage breakdown. But they felt kind of empty in comparison. Like an act. A façade. Something that Tuck-the-jock did to ensure he was the toast of the town, the life of the party.

But three days in bed with Cassie had made him reassess his definition. Okay, there hadn't been a lot of talking, but neither had there been a lot of sexual gymnastics. Mostly they'd just explored each other's bodies. Just touching and stroking and joining together, then drifting to sleep and starting all over again.

But it was the first time he could remember he'd been himself in a long time. Stripped back to the man, not the quarterback, because Cassie didn't have a clue who the footballer was nor did she give a damn. He'd been anonymous for a change.

And *that* had been fun.

Cassie stood very still for a long time after Tuck left, staring at the closed door. *Fun.* No one had ever told her she was fun. Not even as a child. The kids at school had called her brainiac and geek. Her doctor had called her a smart little cookie. Her teachers had said she was a whizz-kid. The university chancellor had called her a once-in-a-generation mind.

She'd never been anyone's *fun* before.

She picked up his card, his scent enveloping her as she brushed it against her mouth. It took all her willpower to toss it in the empty rubbish bin.

Three days later Cassie realised she'd created a monster—or fed one anyway—because her libido was back at full bitch again. The first day had been good. She'd felt focused and invigorated, springing from bed, eager to live the dream. But the next morning her thoughts had returned to the carnal, and slowly things had started to slide until her concentration was shot, her ability to analyse simple data non-existent and her interest had hit an all-time low.

And *everything* reminded her of Tuck. Passing the students hanging out in the hallway. Pulling one of her geek logo shirts over her head. Looking at the images from deep-space telescopes and seeing a pair of starburst-blue eyes.

Her professor had asked her earlier today if everything was okay. *Actually enquired if she was homesick.* As if she was one of the fifteen-year-olds currently running around campus instead of an almost thirty-year-old astronomer with a Mensa-rated IQ studying auroras on Jupiter.

Even now, at nine o'clock at night, sitting at her desk, she looked down at the paper she was reading to find she'd been doodling a certain name in the margins. *Like a teenager!* Not that she'd ever been *that* kind of a teenager.

Cassie squirmed in her chair in disgust, throwing her pen down. But that didn't help as her body was hellbent on betraying her too. The movement stirred internal muscles that were still hypersensitive and sensation rolled through the pit of her belly. The brush of her arms against her nipples had them hard and aching. The same type of ache that had taken up semi-permanent residence between her legs and woke her in the middle of the night.

Cassie reached for the phone to dial Gina. She'd know what to say, what to do. But she withdrew her hand at the last moment, not sure she really wanted to hear her friend's recommendations or—worse—advice about needing to collect more data from Tuck for her libido experiment.

She was a freaking genius, for crying out loud! Her head *would* rule her body.

She threw the paper down and opened her laptop, looking at the latest images they'd received today. Jupiter's auroras were particularly vibrant, and usually just the sheer enormity and random beauty of the solar system was enough to lift her beyond any of the mundane issues of earth. But it wasn't tonight.

Half an hour later she closed the laptop lid, knowing there was really only one solution to her problem. She could feel herself sliding towards an abyss she was all too familiar with and, whether she liked it or not, *the jock* seemed to be her way out.

Okay, she'd told him her brain was back. And it was. She'd told him her libido wouldn't be out of control again. And it wasn't. It just needed one more night.

Maybe he'd be open to one more night?

Mind made up, she scrambled frantically through her wastebasket, her fingers snatching at the card sitting at the very bottom, automatically bringing it to her nose for a long, deep sniff. His lingering pheromones catapulted through her system like a shooting star and any arguments her brain might have made got lost in a sea of stupid.

Her fingers trembled as she rang the number. Her heart thundered as it rang once, twice, three times. Her breath caught in her throat when he picked up and said, 'This is Tuck.'

His voice sounded deep and sexy and deliciously

Texan and her brain powered down. She opened her mouth to say something, anything, but nothing came out.

'Hello?'

Cassie tried again and failed. For crying out loud, she could recite the Magna Carta, the American Declaration of Independence and every single one of Winston Churchill's war speeches word for word and she couldn't say a simple hello?

'Cassiopeia…is that you?'

Still she couldn't get the words to come.

'Cassie!'

His sharp enquiry snapped her out of her daze. 'T…Tuck…I…'

'Cassie? Are you okay?'

There was concern in his voice and she hastened to assure him she was fine. 'Yes, I'm good…fine… I just… I…'

Now she was talking to him she didn't know how to say it. She'd already asked him for sex once—it should be easy. But it wasn't. There was a silence at his end now too, that seemed to stretch interminably.

'Don't move,' he said in her ear. 'I'm coming.' And the receiver clicked.

Cassie was lying awake when the soft knock sounded on her door at exactly one-thirty. She'd spent the last four hours convincing herself he didn't really mean he was coming for her straight away—*tonight*. And how could he possibly get inside the locked dorm? But she didn't know anyone else who would be knocking on her door in the middle of the night.

She padded across the floor, her pulse thrumming so loudly in her head she was afraid she was going to wake the whole dorm. She took a steadying breath as she flipped the lock and turned the knob—to reveal one ex-quarterback standing on her doorstep, oozing pheromones in loose running pants and a T-shirt with some sports logo that stretched nicely over every muscle in his chest.

'Tuck,' she murmured. 'How'd you get in?'

'The RA at the front desk is a Texan,' he muttered, his gaze zeroing in on her mouth. He'd been daydreaming about kissing her like some lovelorn Romeo for the last three days and talk just wasn't on his agenda.

He reached for her, yanking her into his arms, his lips swooping to claim hers as he kicked the door shut behind him. Her mouth opened on a frantic little whimper and she tasted like toothpaste and desperation. He sucked it all in, hauling her up his body, gratified to feel the press of her breasts and the wrap of her legs tight around his waist as he ploughed a path straight to her bed.

And then they were falling back on to it and they were stripping away each other's clothes. Her shirt hit the floor and his followed. Her underwear joined the pile. His running pants and cotton briefs seemed to melt away, and then they were skin on skin, licking and sucking and sniffing and kissing and stroking and stoking until they'd built to a fever-pitch where only the strong, thick thrust of him pounding inside her was enough to satisfy the primal roar in their heads and the even more primal demands of their bodies.

Tuck collapsed on top of her as they both lay spent in

the aftermath. For a moment he couldn't even move. It had been that intense. Then he rolled off her, groaning his bone-deep satisfaction. He hit his head against the wall and then banged his perpetually sore knee as he tried to adjust his too-big frame. He cursed as it twinged painfully.

'You really need a bigger bed,' he panted as he shifted to dispose of the condom, then scooped her up and pulled her half on top of him to accommodate both of them within the narrow confines of the mattress.

Cassie gurgled something unintelligible in response as her body seemed to levitate in the afterglow. When she could string enough words together to make a sentence she raised her head and looked down at him through half-lowered lids. 'You came,' she murmured as a strange sort of peace suffused her.

Tuck grinned. 'So did you.'

She rolled her sleepy eyes at him, then snuggled her cheek against his nearest pec as if he were her own personal pillow.

He smiled and stroked her hair, his own eyes shutting as long sleepless nights combined with a potent sexual malaise drifted them both into a deep slumber.

SEVEN

———

EVERYTHING ACHED WHEN Tuck woke at six the next morning. His back was stiff from the wafer-thin mattress, his knee throbbed, his neck was at an awkward angle and his ankles were sore from his feet hanging over the end of the bed.

But Cassie was warm and pliant, snuggled along the length of him, her hair streaming over his chest, her leg bent at the knee, trapping his thigh, her hand splayed on his abdomen, dangerously close to a part of his anatomy that had been *up* for a while.

Tuck smiled. *Atta-boy.*

Unfortunately he didn't have time this morning to do it justice. He had to get up, get going. He had a meeting with some execs in New York at eleven about the app. But, despite the aches and pains from a night in a bed made for an Oompa-loompa aggravating his injuries from a decade of being regularly slammed for sport, he was reluctant to move.

Soon. He'd go soon.

His gaze drifted around a room quite unlike any other

female dorm room he'd ever been in—his jock status had pretty much seen to it that he could judge from personal experience. Hell, it was unlike *any* female bedroom he'd ever been in. No personalised curtains. No pretty rugs. No flowers or multiple soft stuffed toys or brightly coloured cushions or throws littering surfaces. No pinks, no purples, no pastels. No ornaments, no lava lamps, no photographs of friends or lovers.

It was about as girly as a jail cell.

Still, there were some touches to break up the starkness of the room. A couple of star charts were posted above the desk. Some blown-up photographs of who knew what were stuck to the walls. Stars? Black holes? Galaxies far, far away? Whatever they were, they were captivatingly beautiful in their majesty, and Tuck couldn't think of anything more awesome than having the solar system as your office.

A poster of an eerie green glow being cast over a landscape of white was stuck to one wardrobe door, and on the other what appeared to be a planet with a wispy ring of electric blue light at its pole. Auroras, perhaps?

But it was the large poster taking up the entire back of her door that drew his attention. It was of Barringer Crater in Arizona. He knew that because he'd been obsessed by the fifty-thousand-year-old hole in the ground since he'd been a kid and had been there several times. It was a big brown pockmark in the middle of nowhere, and it seemed an odd, even ugly earthbound addition compared to the beauty of the other celestial decorations.

She stirred and Tuck looked down at her. Her hand on his stomach curled into a light fist, dragging its fingernails deliciously against his skin, and he shut his eyes for a moment enjoying the sensation. As did his erection.

'Morning, sleepyhead,' he said, opening his eyes and dropping a kiss on her hair. He really, really had to get going.

Cassie woke to solid warmth and her nostrils full of Tuck. No thoughts of anything *but* Tuck in her head. 'Hmmm,' she murmured, stretching against him, her eyes slowly drifting open. She smiled as her bird's-eye view down the flat of his stomach ended in the delicious outline of his erection.

'Hmmm,' she said again as her hand slid down his belly and reached for it.

Tuck shut his eyes as her hand closed around him and talons of need clawed deep into his buttocks. He reached down and placed a stilling hand on hers. 'I can't stay. I have a meeting at eleven that I can't get out of.'

'Uh-huh,' Cassie said as she gave his girth a squeeze, her thumb running over its firm head.

Tuck dragged her hand away—that was *not* helping. 'Why,' he asked in an effort to distract her, him and his erection, 'do you have a poster of Barringer Crater on your door?'

Cassie dragged her gaze from his fascinating anatomy and glanced up at him, resting her chin on his pec for a moment. He didn't look as if he was going to be easily dissuaded, and the fact that he knew its actual name rather than calling it Meteor Crater, as it was popularly known, piqued her interest. She sighed, then turned her head towards the door, resting her other cheek on his chest.

'I've always wanted to go there,' she said, eyeing the poster. 'There's one like it in Australia, called Wolfe Creek. My mother took me when I was little so it's a bit of a fascination of mine. The girls and I were going to stop in and visit it on our road trip a decade ago, but then…then there was "the great falling out" and it never happened.'

She turned her head back, resting her chin on his chest again, looking straight into his starburst eyes. Tuck's hand absently stroked the small of her back. There wasn't a lot of room in her single bed and he seemed to take it all up. Her position close to the edge was precarious and his hand at the base of her spine was the only thing anchoring her.

'So I promised myself this time around I'd go and see it. It's my reward for when I complete my three months at Cornell.'

Tuck chuckled. 'Sounds much more sensible than getting wasted at Daytona Beach.'

Cassie nodded, not remotely concerned about being thought of as sensible. She *was* sensible. She never did anything rash or ill-considered.

Except this.

Tuck was the very definition of rash and ill-considered. But surely one blip in almost thirty years was allowable? 'I take it you've been?' she said. 'To Barringer?'

Tuck nodded. 'A few times, actually. The stars out there are amazing.'

'Well, they would be,' Cassie said. 'It's the middle of the dessert. No ambient light. No pollution.'

'Yeah.' Tuck smiled as she got all scientific on him. He

picked up a lock of her hair and let it sift through his fingers. 'So...about last night...'

Cassie dropped her forehead to his chest. 'I'm sorry,' she said, her voice muffled against his pec. She looked up. 'I think my libido went into some kind of...withdrawal situation. I just needed...*it* just needed another night.'

Tuck grinned. 'Another hit, huh?'

Cassie didn't like the idea that she might be addicted to Tuck. She was far too highly evolved for that—even if evidence to the contrary had not been forthcoming of late.

She had to stay in charge of this thing.

'Libido is influenced by a variety of factors often not under conscious control,' she said, trying to give herself an out for her inexplicable behaviour.

'So you may require my *services* again?' Tuck tried to decide whether he cared about being used by a horny PhD student who cared even less about his celebrity status than she did about football. *He didn't.*

Cassie's nipples beaded against his chest at the suggestion, as if it was made from a block of ice instead of hot, pliant muscle. She looked down at his still present erection. Her nostrils flared. Lust surged through her belly.

'Possibly,' she murmured, entranced by the pure masculinity of it, her synapses shorting out as her hand slid down.

'Oh, no, you don't,' Tuck said, grabbing her fingers before they could wreak havoc at their destination. 'I really have to go.'

Cassie glanced at him. 'I'll be quick,' she said, and shimmied down his body, kissing his ribs, his belly button, his hip on her way down.

Tuck shut his eyes as the heat of her mouth closed over him. 'Oh, God, I've created a monster,' he groaned, his eyes shutting as his resistance ebbed beneath her onslaught. He threaded his hands through her hair and surrendered to the pleasure, his appointment forgotten.

When she called him two nights later, asking for just one more night, Tuck hired a helicopter, grateful that his money and celebrity meant he didn't have to endure another eight-hour round trip in his car.

Two nights later he did the same thing. But she hadn't instigated the trip this time, so he was a little nervous when he knocked on her door at ten o'clock.

'One more?' he asked when she opened it.

Her shirt said 'Never drink and derive', and she looked all smart and serious and cute and nerdy, with a pencil tucked behind her ear, and he wanted her so damn bad he didn't even wait for an answer before yanking her into his arms, swivelling her around and using their combined body weight to shut the door, pressing her hard against it as he plundered every millimetre of her mouth.

Hell, they didn't even make it to the bed.

He sure as hell had no idea what delightful underwear logo awaited him, because he just tore it right off in his haste to be inside her. And nothing mattered after that except the crazy, blind, driving need that seemed to grow more desperate every day.

Tuck woke the next morning, every bone, muscle and joint protesting, knowing he would never survive another night on Cassie's mattress.

He was just too old and injured for dorm beds.

Cassie wasn't with him and he raised his head, expecting to see her sitting at her desk or standing by her wardrobe getting dressed. But the room was empty. He looked at his watch. Eight o'clock. Given how late it had been when they'd eventually gone to sleep, he wasn't surprised he'd slept in.

But when had she left?

Tuck unfolded himself from the bed, his body aching as he stood slowly and headed to the pile of clothes by the door that he didn't even remember losing last night. He bent over and both knees twinged. He climbed into his shorts and pulled his T-shirt over his head. A scrap of fabric remained on the floor and he picked it up, grinning at what was left of Cassie's underwear and its amusing logo: *Vacancy: Rocket Scientists need only apply.*

He walked to her desk and tossed them in the bin. And that was when he saw the note propped up by a couple of textbooks. He opened it, and the first line jumped out at him.

We can't keep doing this, Tuck.

Well, she was damn right about that. Her bed just wasn't made for two.

I'm getting nothing done. I can't concentrate. And all I do is think about you. I think it's best if I go cold turkey.

I know that with hard work, focus and medication my libido will have to eventually submit to the dictates of a higher power. It has been my dream to come to Cornell, a much desired step in a grander plan, and I ask that you not derail that. Or, given that you are so much more practised at this than I, let me derail it either. If I call, please ignore me. No one's ever died from sexual deprivation and I don't expect I'll be the first. It has, as you say, been fun, but it's over.

Tuck read the note several times. Even the way she wrote, so precise and matter-of-fact, cracked him up, and he found his grin getting broader with each read-through.

She was right, of course. What they were doing was utterly distracting and not very productive. He had some work backed up on the app that he'd been neglecting. So ending it—whatever the hell *it* was—would be one solution. But suddenly he had a much better one. He scrunched up the note and threw it in the bin.

He had a busy day ahead of him. He needed breakfast and a plan.

Two hours later he was sitting in the very posh offices of a property rental agency, talking to a very attractive woman about finding him an upmarket serviced apartment in Ithica for him to move into immediately.

Of course he could have done it himself—got a phone book and rung around. But in his experience it was best to outsource these things to an expert who knew the local market and had an eye for class.

The brassy blonde called Abigail fitted the docket perfectly. It helped that she knew who he was, although she was careful not to fawn, which told him she was used to dealing with the higher end of the market. Even so he was more than aware from her subtle body language that she'd be first in line to volunteer should he need company in his bed whilst in Ithica.

The problem was she just didn't do it for him. She should have. She was exactly his type—blonde, well put together, and a cougar to boot. Tuck liked cougars. They weren't usually out for anything other than a good time and a few hours of action between the sheets. If they could bag a celebrity that was just the cherry on the cake for them.

But, surprisingly, over the course of a week his type had changed.

Her eyes were artfully made up, with perfectly arched brows, but they didn't glitter with intelligence or hold the secrets of the universe. Her hair fell in a fluffy cloud around her head and shoulders and reeked of a posh salon, but he'd bet his last dime she couldn't go three hours without brushing it, let alone three whole days full of head-banging, style-destroying sex.

And then there were her...assets. They were nicely on display and, hell, Tuck had always appreciated a nice rack—but he realised there was a certain degree of titillation in having to check things out thoroughly to find the good stuff.

And he knew just the woman who fitted the bill. His new type. And it wasn't Abigail.

She was, however, exceedingly efficient, and within

an hour she had located the perfect place for him in a quiet tree-lined neighbourhood a ten-minute walk from campus. Tuck took a taxi to the posh low-rise and spent all afternoon making phone calls to set himself up for the next three months.

Even if Cassie was resistant to moving in with him—and he had to admit it seemed kind of crazy after only a week—he'd slept his last night in that god-awful dorm bed. She could stay on campus if she really wanted, but if she called in the middle of the night again, wanting him, he'd be sending a car for her.

From now on any and all naked action would be taking place on the cloud-like comfort of a pillow-top mattress.

At six o'clock his wardrobe and his home office, which his PA had packed up and put on an Ithica-bound chopper, arrived, and he spent the next hour setting up. He unpacked the suitcases of clothes and set up his office in the spare bedroom, leaving the desk area in the master bedroom for Cassie's stuff.

Relocating his life was no big deal when the constraints of the everyday—like a job and a budget—were non-existent, and for that Tuck was grateful. It didn't matter where he was—he could do what he did anywhere. As long as he had access to Cassie.

It was just after seven when he was done. He knew Cassie often didn't get back to the dorm until after eight, so he jumped in the car he'd rented and bought enough groceries to fill the fridge. Lucky for Cassie he was an awesome cook, and he whipped up a quick pasta meal for them both before girding his loins and heading back to the dorm.

Cassie recognised Tuck's voice as soon as she entered the dorm, holding court as he was in the lounge area to a group of rapt teenagers. No big surprise, really. She was beginning to think she would recognise his voice underwater amidst a pod of whales.

Her pulse skipped a little. Hadn't he got her note? She couldn't decide whether the feeling in the pit of her stomach was anger or relief. Whether she was mad at him or likely to tear all his clothes off in front of impressionable teenagers.

God knew, she'd thought about nothing else all day.

She shook her head. Just over a week ago she hadn't had any indecision about her emotions. Her life, her feelings—should she have had any—had been completely cut and dry. And then along came Tuck. And her brain had gone into hiding!

She felt a momentary quiver of something that felt a lot like anxiety. She recognised it from those troubled teen years, before medication had helped her control a brain that sped constantly ahead.

She pushed it away on a hard swallow.

'Cassie.' Tuck stood as he spotted her. 'Okay, guys.' He apologised as he prepared to leave, despite the protests. 'Gotta go now.'

He caught up with Cassie outside her door, searching through her bag for her key. 'Evening, ma'am,' he murmured near her ear, low and drawn-out, just as he knew she liked. The falter in her brisk activity was satisfying.

'I left you a note,' Cassie said as his pheromones embraced her and she shut her eyes to resist them. She fitted her key in the lock and opened the door.

Tuck followed her into her room. 'I got it,' he said.

Cassie folded her arms, because they were aching for him and she just didn't trust her body when she no longer understood it. She glared at him. 'This is not cold turkey.'

Tuck smiled at her cranky face. Her eyebrows were drawn together and she was looking at him like mould under a microscope. But he could see the telltale signs giving her away. The flutter of the pulse in the hollow of her throat, the slight flare of her nostrils, the beading of her nipples which, thanks to her folded arms, he could see clearly.

'I had a better idea.'

'It doesn't look like it from where I'm standing,' she said.

'I rented an apartment. It's ten minutes' walk from here and I think you should move in with me.'

Cassie blinked. Had she heard right or had he finally dumbed her down enough that she'd surpassed stupid and slipped right on to crazy?

'Just think about it,' Tuck said, jumping into the silence, holding up his hands as if he was expecting her to attack at any minute. 'It's logical, really.'

Yeah, he knew that was a low blow, considering the plan was three-quarters insane. But he knew he had to make a logical argument.

'You said in your note that you couldn't concentrate. And that all you could think about was me. I'm proposing that living with me will give you the best of both worlds. No need for cold turkey. If I was here all the time, if you had access to me all the time, you wouldn't have to spend all day thinking about *not* having access to me. You'd know I was here to come home to.'

Cassie, who had been girding her loins to throw him out—preferably without ravishing him first—considered what he was saying.

'Part of the problem the last week has been that you've been denying your urges until they've built up and up and your libido is at screaming point. If I was here all the time they wouldn't have to build. Your libido could calm down.'

Cassie remembered the days when her libido had been non-existent. *The good old days.* 'I was hoping that my libido might have...had its fill by now.'

'Well, libidos can be tricky things. Sometimes these things can take a while to burn out.'

Wasn't that just what Gina had said? 'How long's a while?' she demanded. 'Define it.'

Tuck shook his head solemnly. 'Well, that's not easily definable—there are too many variables.' Tuck wasn't above a bit of geek-talk to sway her his way. 'It could be a week. It could be your entire three months at Cornell. That's a long time with shot concentration.' Tuck shoved his hands into the pockets of his track pants. '*Very* unproductive.'

Cassie didn't like the sound of that. Maybe a 'calm' libido was the best she could hope for while this thing *burnt itself out,* as Tuck had put it. It certainly wasn't showing any sign of abating yet if the very powerful urge to kiss him currently playing havoc with her will-power was anything to go by.

'Why not give it a trial run?' he suggested. 'I think you'll find it beneficial to your concentration, but if you don't...' Tuck shrugged. 'You can always come back here.'

Cassie had to admit it did sound logical. A trial. Another experiment. She had no doubt that he was manipulating her lifelong obsession with logic, but that didn't mean he wasn't right. And, more than ever, she needed logic in her life.

Cassie nodded. 'Okay. Agreed. Can you get my suit-case down from the top of the wardrobe?'

It was Tuck's turn to blink. He'd thought it was going to be much more difficult than that. He had arguments stacked up that he'd been rehearsing for hours.

'Well?' Cassie said as she looked at a stationary Tuck. 'Are we going or not?'

Tuck grinned. 'Yes, ma'am.'

And it worked brilliantly. Tuck had been right. Knowing he was there to come home to freed up all her head space and she was finally able to get into her work. Sure, she got a little spacey towards the end of the day, when her libido was obviously starting to run a little low on its Tuck hit, but Cassie was so productive she was almost delirious with it.

Having a constant supply of sex also meant more sleep, which Cassie knew was a major requirement of her overactive brain. Instead of days of famine which had kept her awake and hungry, followed by a night of feasting which had kept her awake and sated, she had a constant source of fuel and something more potent than sleeping tablets to get her off to sleep.

Not that she would ever stop taking them. She might be on top, but the memories of a time when she hadn't been still burned brightly and she relied on the pills to help her maintain her mental balance.

Still, things were good. Way better than Cassie would have ever thought possible. And if every now and then the thought that she was *living with a man* confused her logic she put it in the 'too hard' basket along with her libido and concentrated on her work.

Their first Sunday morning together threw up the first potential hurdle, and it came from out of the blue. Tuck had been out after an early round of sex and bought every paper he could lay his hands on. It was a bit of a Sunday morning ritual for him, and Cassie was content to sit with him, eating the omelette he'd made, and work her way through the papers too.

'Why'd you get this one?' she asked, holding up a tabloid well known for bizarre stories on alien life and other things belonging in the realm of the wild and whacky.

Tuck looked up from a sports section. 'Force of habit. It's amazing how much you find out about yourself in the pages of a tabloid.'

Cassie raised an eyebrow. 'I think that's called narcissism,' she said as she flicked to the second page.

Tuck grinned. 'No. It's called protecting my reputation.' He turned his attention back to the college ball scores as he said, 'Plus I know who to sic my lawyer on.'

Cassie shook her head, her gaze falling on a particularly startling headline. 'Do you mean like this?' she asked, holding it up for him to see. '"Tuck is my Baby Daddy"'.

Tuck's head snapped up as the blazing bold headline jumped out at him. His NFL official photograph was there, along with a picture of a vaguely familiar busty blonde woman with a toddler on her hip. 'What the...?' he said as he stood and headed to her side of the table.

'Do you know someone called Jenny Jones?' Cassie asked as she scanned the article.

Tuck leaned on Cassie's chair, rage building inside him as he read over her shoulder. Sure, he remembered Jenny. He'd spent two nights with her in Vegas just after his divorce was final.

'Yeah.' Tuck's jaw clenched. 'I know her.' He reached for his phone and stalked to the bay windows that looked down onto the street.

'Who are you ringing?' she asked.

'My lawyer.'

It went to voicemail and Tuck left a terse message about the amount of money he was paying him and how he expected to hear from him in the next ten minutes.

'It's a lie,' he said, turning to face Cassie. He couldn't believe the bare-faced audacity of the paper to print such a wild, unsubstantiated claim. Generally his management would have been asked for comment, given a heads-up, but sometimes rags like this didn't bother with clarification.

He was going to sue their goddamned asses off. They were going to be sorry they'd *ever* screwed with him.

Cassie blinked at Tuck's vehemence. He started to pace, his fists curled, his face stony. 'So you don't know her?' she said, tracking his restless prowl. 'You didn't sleep with her?'

'Oh, I know her,' Tuck said, abruptly halting his pacing. 'And I slept with her. Exactly as she claims in the article.'

'So...you *could* be the father?' Cassie said. It seemed logical to her.

Tuck shook his head emphatically. 'No.'

Cassie frowned. 'You used condoms?'

'Yes, we did. I *always* use condoms.'

'You know they only have a ninety-nine percent accuracy, right? Statistically it is still possible—'

'It's not possible,' Tuck interrupted.

'Well, there is a one percent—'

'No,' Tuck interrupted again. 'It's *not* possible.' He shoved his hand through his hair. 'I'm infertile. Probably have been most of my life. "Idiopathic", they call it. Which just means they don't know what the hell's caused it. But they suspect it was a virus that laid me low when I was eighteen...totally screwed up my season too. Trust me—I can tell you, for sure that I couldn't get a woman pregnant if she was the most fertile female on the planet. Which is kind of ironic, considering the number of paternity tests I've faced over the years.'

'How long have you known?' she asked.

'I found out when April and I tried to get pregnant.'

It had been a particularly nasty whammy, on top of the recurrent knee injury screwing with his career. Nothing like being a dud at everything—quarterback, husband, man.

Cassie didn't know what to say. With absolutely no

desire to have children herself, she didn't understand the drive. But she could see that Tuck was gutted by it. 'I'm...sorry,' she said.

The phone rang then, and Tuck answered immediately. Cassie listened to the one-sided conversation. Although perhaps *rant* was a better word. Tuck was steamed, and she wasn't sure she'd ever heard that many four-letter words.

Tuck ended the call and threw the phone on the table in disgust.

'I take it this happens a lot?'

He nodded. 'This will be the eighth paternity claim against me.' He raked a hand through his hair. 'Sorry, you probably don't need this. But I can assure you it's not true.'

Cassie frowned. 'No need to apologise. Nothing to do with me.'

Tuck blinked. He'd been with women in the past when these accusations had come at him and they'd been spitting mad. Cassie just sat there, looking at him all nonplussed, and he couldn't help but laugh. 'You're the only woman I know that wouldn't have a hissy fit over this.'

'It's not really my business, is it?' She shrugged.

'Well, most women in your position would think it *was* their business.'

'They would?'

Tuck nodded. 'They'd be kind of pissed.'

'Because of the jealousy thing?' Cassie asked.

Tuck laughed again. 'Ahh...yup. Most women want me to marry *them* and give *them* lots of little quarterbacks. They'd be *more* than annoyed that someone else was trying to claim that place in my life.'

Cassie thought about that for a moment. She supposed human jealousy and other less evolved emotions might come into play here—but not with her.

'But I don't want to marry you,' she said. 'And I don't want to have your babies. I'm here for three months, then I'm going back to Australia, and next year I'm going to Antarctica. And all of the years after that are going to be dedicated to my career which, as my mother could tell you, is not family-friendly. This is just a libido thing, remember?'

Bloody hell—she was hard on a man's ego. An ego that had already suffered a few hard years with the triple blow of a tanking career, a crumbling marriage and infertility. And just when he was on the up Jenny came along to sink in the boot.

The fact that Cassie wanted nothing from him other than a little libido-taming sounded damn good to him. And most of all it was honest. She was the only woman who had ever been straight with him about what she wanted—not even April had been honest about that.

And *damn* if that didn't feel good.

EIGHT

———

THE FOLLOWING WEEK Reese called as Cassie walked to the apartment after a full day at the Earth Sciences building. The campus was a virtual ghost town, with most of the summer students heading home for the looming Fourth of July celebrations. Cassie understood the importance of the holiday to Americans, but it was annoying to be losing a day at the university when she was finally back on track with her studies.

After some preliminary chit-chat about Cornell and the PhD, and Reese and Mason's state of bliss, Reese said, 'So, Mason and I are having a big Fourth thing here, and we were hoping you could hop on a bus tomorrow and come join us.'

Ordinarily Cassie would have said yes. She'd missed Reese, and although she had kept in touch over the years it was a novelty for them to be in the same country!

'Can't,' she said. 'Tuck has plans for me.'

'Tuck?'

'Yes,' Cassie said. 'Some big surprise he's arranged.'

'*My* Tuck?' Reese clarified. 'You're...still seeing each other?'

'Uh-huh.' There was silence at the end of the line for a moment, and Cassie realised maybe this news was the type of thing that *gal pals* shared with each other. 'Sort of.'

'Sort of?'

'Well, it's not like that. I mean, it *is*...but... It's just a libido thing. It's just...sex. I only moved in with him for the sex.'

'You *moved in* with him?'

Cassie held the phone away from her ear as Reese's squeak reverberated loudly around her ear canal.

'Okay,' Reese said. 'Whoever this is, stop goofing around and put my friend Cassie on. My friend Cassie with a mega-brain, who lives and breathes astronomy and *does not* shack up with a man she met not even a month ago. Who doesn't *shack up* period!'

'Funny,' Cassie murmured, holding the phone slightly away from her ear as Reese's voice became more and more shrill.

'Cassie...honey...this is completely out of character for you...'

'I know that,' Cassie said. 'But my work was suffering. All I could do was think about him...it was so...*dumb!* Then Tuck got a place at Ithica and suggested how logical it was that I move in—'

Reese snorted. 'I bet he did.'

Cassie shook her head vehemently. 'No, he was right. This way I get to satisfy my brain *and* my libido.'

'Win-win,' Reese said.

'Exactly,' Cassie agreed.

There was some more silence before Reese spoke again. 'Honey...Tuck's my cousin, and I love him, but... he can be a bit of a...hound dog. Just look at this latest news about that woman in Vegas.'

'It's not his baby, Reese.'

'Oh...are the paternity results in already?'

'He doesn't need them,' Cassie said. 'He's infertile. He found out when he and April were trying to get pregnant.'

'Oh, no,' Reese gasped. 'Poor Tuck. I didn't know that. I knew he was going through a hard time a few years back, but I didn't realise...'

Cassie stopped and waited at a pedestrian light. 'He's fine,' she dismissed.

'Are you sure? Tuck's always had a pretty big ego, and most men's identities *are* wrapped up in things like their jobs and their virility. To have someone popping up and throwing his inabilities in his face... I don't know. It has to be a blow...'

The light changed and Cassie crossed the road. 'Well, he sicced his lawyer on to it with great delight and hasn't mentioned it since, so...'

'Men don't, though...they brood and bury it. Just look at how screwed up Mason was. It's not very healthy. Have you asked him about it?'

'No.' Cassie felt a pang. Was Reese right? *Was* Tuck bothered by this more than he was letting on? 'Should I have?'

Was *she* supposed to do something about it?

This was why she preferred science. It made sense. She knew what do with it.

'No, no...' Reese assured her. 'Anyway, I have to go, but maybe Mason and I could come to Ithica next weekend for a visit? I'll have probably wrapped my head around the whole Cassie-living-with-a-man thing by then. Maybe we can all get together? I'll see what Gina and Marnie are doing.'

Cassie hung up a minute later, the apartment in her sights. But for the first time in three weeks the spring in her step was missing.

'You're quiet,' Tuck said an hour later as he picked up their plates and headed for the kitchen.

Normally Cassie was full of the day's developments, where she was at with the project, or the latest thing of beauty a telescope had captured somewhere in outer space. But tonight she'd eaten and let him do most of the talking.

Cassie opened her mouth to deny it, but then she realised he was right. She'd been preoccupied with what Reese had said and trying to puzzle out what was expected of her. If this whole thing with Jenny had suddenly brought Tuck's infertility to the fore and he was feeling somehow less...*masculine,* was it her role to restore his sense of worth?

Was she supposed to get him talking about it? Give him an avenue for discussion? Did he need his hand held? His ego stroked?

Should she have asked him about it?

Argh! She'd never felt this inept in her life. Where was Gina when she needed her?

'Reese thinks that this paternity thing may be magnifying a sense of injured masculinity stemming from your infertility and that you may be brooding and burying your feelings in an unhealthy way,' she blurted out.

Tuck blinked. 'You told Reese about my infertility?'

Cassie shrugged. 'I assumed she already knew,' she said matter-of-factly. She missed the tightening at the angle of his jaw as she ploughed on. 'Is she right?'

Tuck turned to face the sink and flicked the hot water tap on. 'Reese should mind her own damn business.'

Cassie stared at Tuck's back. Right, then. That seemed a fairly definitive *stay-out-of-it* to her. Except she knew enough about social interaction to know that words and actions could often contradict.

She stood and headed towards him. 'If she is, I was thinking maybe I could...help you through it.' *Somehow...* 'Like the way you're helping *me* with my libido issues.'

Tuck turned back and smiled at her, a gleam in his eyes. 'Oh, you're helping.'

'I am?'

'Sure—nothing like a steady supply of great sex to soothe a man's ego.'

So his ego *was* bent out of shape? She pulled up at the other side of the bench. 'I think that might be the unhealthy part.'

Tuck leaned his butt against the sink. 'I don't know about you, but I've never felt more healthy.'

Cassie had to admit, as every cell in her body purred beneath the blast of sexual energy arcing between them, that the man made a good point. But this hadn't exactly been the easiest thing for her to do, and she wouldn't let him, or her libido, derail her from her objective.

'Tuck. I'm trying to...to be sensitive to your...issues...'

Tuck was momentarily stunned, and then he laughed. 'Well, look at you,' he teased. 'Going all Dr Feelgood on me.'

'Tuck.'

He sobered. 'I'm fine.' He turned back to the sink. 'I was married, my career tanked, we couldn't have a baby and then I wasn't married any more.'

'Two years isn't very long,' she said to his beautiful broad back. Even her parents, who lived in a strange kind of separate togetherness, had managed thirty years.

Tuck shrugged. 'I doubt anyone was surprised. We'd only known each other for a few months before we got hitched.'

Cassie tried to absorb the enormity of such an impulsive act. It seemed as crazy as Reese falling for Mason in a week all those years ago. Or Gina sleeping with the betrothed Carter.

And just as unfathomable.

'That seems a little rash,' she said.

Tuck stared at the suds covering his hands. It *had* been rash, but at the time it had seemed so damn right. He turned again, shoving one soapy hand on his hip. Cassie was looking at him cluelessly, her eyebrows scrunched together in a frown, a pencil behind her ear. He doubted she'd understand his state of absolute desperation in her world of crystal-clear logic.

But he suddenly wanted her to.

'She was a nurse where I was having my physical therapy. I'd been through several operations and my career was stalled, she was young and sweet and adorable, and I felt old and clapped-out and impotent. She believed in me in a way that wasn't fake like so many others around me and I *needed* that. Football was all I had. It was all I knew.'

He raked a hand through his hair, angry at himself still for taking all her youth and sweetness and sucking it out of her as his career spiralled downwards.

'When she wanted a baby it seemed like the one thing I *could* give her—because the glamorous life of an athlete's wife hadn't exactly been rainbows and unicorns. And, even though part of me knew that bringing a kid into the crumbling mix of our marriage would be stupid, she loved me and I was *trying* to hold on to that. To have one part of my life going right. It seemed like a way to hold us together.'

Cassie frowned. 'For a smart man that was a really dumb move.'

Tuck gave a short, sharp laugh. Trust Cassie to tell it like it was. 'I don't know... It might have been okay if I'd loved her like she'd loved me, if we'd got pregnant. But we couldn't...and when we found out that it was me...it was my fault...it hit me worse than the tackle that gave me a concussion during my first Super Bowl. I mean, I was the *QB*, I was *the man*...and then I wasn't. I couldn't be a father and I couldn't play football either, so what was I?'

Cassie could hear the anguish twisting his words and knew it was her turn to say something. Her role to make it better. Her social awkwardness closed in around her. 'I don't think your...ability to father a child defines you any more than your ability to kick a football around.'

Tuck crossed his arms. 'It sure didn't feel like it at the time. I think I spent a lot of time *defining* myself as a right SOB for a while there.'

'And now? With football and babies off the table?' she asked.

'Not much point wanting something you can't have, is there? Football is over, and I've come to terms with that. And to be honest I'm not really sure I want a kid anyway.' He shrugged. 'I've moved on.'

'For what it's worth, I don't much care about having kids either.'

Tuck chuckled. 'And that's what I like about you. So you can assure Reese I'm just fine. That my *masculinity*...' he dropped his gaze to her breasts '...is just fine.'

Cassie swallowed. *Oh, yes, indeed it was.*

Tuck's mobile rang later that night, just as he finished Skyping with a software engineer about the app. If it had been anyone else other than Dylan he wouldn't have answered. The shower had just been turned on and a wet, naked Cassie was exactly what he needed after a day of dealing with lawyer crap—and their conversation earlier had roused old hurts.

But he'd spoken so little to his best friend since Reese had jilted him a month ago he knew he had to take the call. They chatted for a while about the wash-up from the wedding-that-wasn't, and Tuck was satisfied that

Dylan really seemed okay, and they chatted about the most recent paternity allegations against Tuck.

'So...' Dylan said. 'Reese called me earlier.'

'Ah,' Tuck said. His meddling cousin *had* been a busy little beaver, hadn't she? 'Don't you think it's odd to be taking phone calls from the woman who so recently jilted you?'

'Nice try at deflection, buddy. But you know Reese is worried that Cassie will get hurt.'

Tuck frowned. So this wasn't about him and his masculinity. It was about Cassie. And Reese was sending her ex-fiancé to do her dirty work. 'Reese should know that Cassie is not the kind to emotionally invest. She's just having fun. Blowing off some steam. We both are.'

'Right...but maybe you want to think about not getting involved for a while? Let the dust settle from this Jenny thing? Trust me, you don't die from celibacy.'

'It's fine, Dylan,' Tuck assured him. 'It's the perfect relationship. She's not some groupie. She doesn't want to marry me *or* have my babies. Which is just as well, considering...'

Tuck had tried not to make that sound bitter, but Dylan was the only person other than April, a couple of doctors and apparently now Reese who knew the truth, and this week in particular his infertility had come back to haunt him.

'She's here for three months, bro, and I'm her drug of choice,' he hastened to add. 'It's a temporary thing. It's...symbiotic.'

Dylan laughed. 'Symbiotic? She turning you into a scientist too?'

Tuck laughed too. 'Just getting my geek on.'

'She doesn't really strike me as your...type.'

Tuck shrugged. 'I think I'm getting myself a new type.'

'Okay...'

'No, I mean it,' Tuck said. 'She's amazing, you know. She has all this serious geek thing going on, and she walks around with this pencil behind her ear all the time, and it's so damn cute. But underneath it all she's incredibly passionate. And she doesn't do any of that clingy, needy stuff—'

'I thought,' Dylan butted in, 'you *liked* them clingy?'

Tuck had to admit that up until now that had been true. He'd liked being the *big man*, squiring around his women, treating them like princesses no matter how brief their acquaintance. But that had been the role his celebrity, a string of eager women and examples from his peers had forced him into early in his dating career, setting up an unhealthy pattern.

Cassie's independence had been a breath of fresh air.

Tuck grinned. 'Apparently not.'

There was silence for a moment or two, then Dylan said, 'Are you...are you *serious* about her?'

'Nah.' Tuck laughed, pushing the feeling that Cassie was already under his skin aside. 'It's just fun, Dylan. She's using me. I'm letting her. Win-win.'

'Just...be careful, okay? And by that I mean look out for you too.'

'Aww, buddy, are we going to hug now?'

'Okay. I'm going to hang up.'

'Good, I have a naked woman in a shower waiting for me.'

Dylan snorted. 'Celibacy rocks. You should try it.'

Tuck laughed. 'Whatever gets you through the night.'

One minute later he'd shed his clothes, stepped into the cubicle, and his hands were sliding onto Cassie's wet hips and heading north.

Celibacy rocks, his ass.

Cassie looked down at the arid landscape far below. Tuck's Gulf Stream had been flying since six a.m. and it was now midday.

'When are you going to tell me where we're going?' she asked Tuck as he placed a tray with a selection of gourmet subs cut into small portions on the table between them.

Tuck sat opposite her and grinned. 'You'll know when we get there.'

Cassie didn't like surprises. There was no logic to them at all. 'Fine,' she said as she selected the closest portion. 'Can you tell me how much longer we'll be flying?'

'Another hour or so,' he said, then bit into his sub.

As Cassie had no idea in which direction they were flying—although it was obviously some kind of west—the ETA didn't really help to ascertain their whereabouts, but at least she had a timeframe in her head. She liked to *know* things. When she set out every day for work she already knew in her head what the day would be like. It didn't mean she couldn't be flexible, should something crop up out of the blue, it was just logical and time-effective to have a systematic plan.

They ate quietly for a few minutes, with Tuck's gaze

never leaving her face. His eyes kept dropping to her mouth, and it was disconcerting that something so mundane could kick her libido into overdrive.

She was beginning to think this thing would *never* burn itself out!

'So,' she said, looking around the plane's interior, desperate for some conversation to divert the blood pooling between her thighs back to her brain. 'I guess this means you're seriously rich, huh?'

Tuck stopped chewing for a moment at her bald statement. Then he laughed, and then coughed as he almost inhaled his lunch. Most women had *that* sized up within a few minutes and then spent the entire time trying to spend as much of his money as possible. It was a novelty to be with someone who didn't seem to care. In fact, by the look on her face, it would seem this was the first time his wealth had actually sunk in:

'I've done all right for myself,' he said, after she'd passed him a bottle of water and he'd gulped down a couple of mouthfuls.

Tuck waited for her to ask him to clarify how well he'd done, or to ask how much the plane had cost. Instead she said, 'I've never been in a plane this small.'

Tuck shook his head and chuckled.

Cassie frowned. 'What?'

'Nothing...I've just never met a woman like you.'

'I'd be surprised if you had,' she said. 'Female astronomers with a genius IQ are pretty thin on the ground.'

He laughed again. 'No...I mean so oblivious to material things.'

Cassie shrugged. 'Human beings really only have five basic requirements. The rest is just...*stuff*.'

'Makes you kind of hard to impress,' he joked.

Cassie raised an eyebrow at him. 'I think your ability to give me screaming orgasms every night, night after night, is pretty impressive.'

Her words, delivered in that non-flirty, matter-of-fact tone of hers, crawled right inside his pants and stroked. He was used to being appreciated for his 'stuff' and it was a turn-on to be appreciated for his innate talents. He felt as if he was standing under the lights again, football in hand, listening to the crowd screaming his name.

The last few years had been generally emasculating—Cassie's unconditional presence in his life made him feel virile and potent again.

'You make a hell of an argument.' He smiled. 'But I think you need to prepare yourself to be pretty damn impressed when this plane lands. And I'm going to do it without even touching you.'

Cassie stood in the open doorway of the Gulf Stream an hour later, looking out into the glare of a hot dry day for a clue as to their location. Then she saw the sign proclaiming their destination—Flagstaff, Arizona. Her heart skipped a beat. She turned to look at Tuck, who loomed behind her.

'We're going to Barringer?'

Tuck grinned. 'Yup.'

Cassie was momentarily speechless. She'd had no idea when Tuck had asked her to pack an overnight bag last night where they'd end up, but this would have been her very last guess. She turned back to look at the sign again.

It was perfect. He couldn't have picked a more perfect destination to bring her to.

'I...I don't know what to say.' She looked back at him. 'Thank you, Tuck. Thank you so much. This is totally...'

She didn't have words. And it was hard to speak anyway as a bloom of heat in her chest travelled upwards, threatening to close off her throat.

'Impressive?' he supplied.

Cassie nodded. He looked so cocky and sure of himself, knowing how very much it meant to her, and all scruffy and casual. His pheromones oozed all over her and that heat spread everywhere. *He was sexy when he was right.*

She launched herself into his arms, her mouth seeking his, wanting to smell him, taste him, absorb him into her. Her tongue sought his and he groaned against her mouth, his hands splaying low on the small of her back, holding her steady, anchoring them together as ardour swayed them both in the narrow doorway.

'Wow—that impressive, huh?' he teased when she finally let go of him. Her spontaneity was as sexy as hell for someone who didn't really *do* spontaneity.

Cassie felt a little light-headed for a moment, clinging to his biceps all warm and bulky in her palms. 'You did good.'

He smiled and gestured for her to precede him. 'Well, let's get going, then.'

* * *

After that the afternoon flew by. Despite it being a holiday, a vintage Cadillac Deville convertible was waiting for them at the airport, because apparently an American road trip called for an American classic even if it only took them twenty minutes to arrive at their destination.

Cassie felt a little trill of happiness as she bounded out of the car. It increased when she looked at Tuck. The only thing he could have done that was more perfect was fly her to the moon, but she guessed even Tuck had his limitations.

Not to mention those nights when he'd taken her closer to the stars than any deep-space telescope ever had...

There were quite a few visitors bustling in and out of the Visitor Center, and Cassie hurried quickly in its direction, impatient to see the crater. She wasn't disappointed. The site of the massive hole in the earth, four thousand feet across, stopped her in its tracks. It was simply awe-inspiring, and Cassie just stood and stared at it, her astronomer's heart just about bursting out of her chest, trying to wrap her head around the circumstances of its creation.

'You're excited, right?' Tuck murmured low in her ear.

Cassie dug him in the ribs, but her face felt flushed, her pulse tripped, she was hyperaware—it *was* a tiny bit sexual. 'I wish you'd told me,' she said, turning to face him. 'I don't have my camera with me.'

Tuck held up a bag that held a very expensive piece of photographic gear that he'd figured would impress even a woman who had access to kick-ass telescopes on a daily basis.

Cassie grabbed him by his shirt and smacked a brief, hard kiss on his mouth. 'You are outdoing yourself today.'

Tuck grinned. 'Oh, there's more where that came from, baby.'

But Cassie barely heard him, distracted as she was by the path skirting the rim of the crater. If she'd been allowed, she would have jumped over the edge and dashed to the bottom. It looked like a lunar surface, hallowed ground, and to walk where the Apollo astronauts had trained would be a dream come true.

'There's a rim tour starting in ten minutes,' Tuck said.

'We'll catch the next one,' she said, because she was impatient but also because she didn't want to hear someone else's patter first. She just wanted to absorb everything and match it with the reams of knowledge teeming in her head.

Tuck chuckled. 'Okay, lead on.'

They spent two hours in the blazing sun, stopping and starting and reading information boards and taking pictures. Cassie talked geek stuff about asteroids and took pictures, and Tuck enjoyed her breadth of knowledge mixed with her infectious excitement. He'd never seen her so animated and he liked it.

Then they joined a tour for another go around the rim, which wasn't anywhere near as exciting—mainly because it took the group of twenty only about two minutes to recognise Tuck, and he spent a lot of time as they went around talking about himself to a bunch of fans and not next to Cassie as he'd wanted.

They stopped at one of the viewing areas and Cassie looked over at Tuck, talking to a couple of teenagers. He shot her an apologetic shrug and she just smiled and rolled her eyes. The guide was talking about the make-up of the asteroid that had slammed into the earth and Cassie separated herself slightly to snap another picture down into the crater.

A man holding a camera sidled up beside her and said, 'Magnificent, isn't it?'

Cassie looked away from the viewfinder. 'Oh, yes,' she breathed. 'Truly amazing.' She looked through the lens again.

'You're with Tuck, yes?' he asked casually. 'You his...?' He looked her up and down. 'Girlfriend?'

Cassie glanced at him. The guy was looking at her as if he was trying to figure out what genus and species she belonged to. He had a huge gold ring on his finger and a heavy gold chain around his neck. And a very large, ex-pensive-looking camera with a gigantic lens. Tuck would have said he was compensating for something.

'Not really.'

What else could she say? *No, he's just my libido's drug of choice?* Hardly something you'd tell a stranger, even if it was the very startling truth. Plus, after today she wasn't sure what she felt about him. It suddenly seemed more than just sex between them. But maybe that was just the crater talking?

The guy was still watching her closely, and Cassie glanced over to see Tuck signing another autograph. She turned her attention back to the camera, snapping off more pictures.

'You're not his usual...type.'

Cassie's finger faltered on the button. She was wearing a pair of roomy gym shorts that allowed a good flow of air in the stifling heat and her usual three-sizes-too-big T-shirt that said *'Higgs Boson Gives Me a Hadron'*. Tuck had bought her a baseball cap from the gift shop and squashed it down on her head before the tour had started. Her dark brown hair hung down her back in its usual low ponytail, held fast by a floral scrunchie.

Her cheeks were flushed pink from the heat and she had sweat on her upper lip and forehead. She looked at the man over the top of the camera.

'They usually wear...' he looked over her outfit again, as if he was some Parisian designer who did not like what he saw '...less. And have more...make-up.'

Cassie frowned at the completely impractical observation. 'Who wears make-up in this heat?'

Then a little boy ran up to him, saying, 'Daddy, Daddy.'

'Hey, Zack,' he said.

'Look, I got Tuck's autograph.'

And then the guide moved them on and the conversation was over as the guy was dragged back to his family and Tuck headed her way.

'More pictures?' Tuck asked.

His hand slid onto her neck under the knot of her ponytail and Cassie smiled up at him. 'Can't wait to see these on my laptop,' she said.

Tuck kissed the tip of her nose and they moved on with the rest of the tour.

They stayed until the crater closed at five, and then drove into Flagstaff and wandered about the town centre, enjoying the Fourth of July celebrations. Tuck regaled Cassie with stories of his family's legendary Texan celebrations.

'Oh, look, they've got fireworks later,' Cassie said as she bit into an enormous stick of fairy floss—or cotton candy, as Tuck had told her.

'Oh, no. I have plans for you,' Tuck said, his arm around her waist, drawing her close into his side as they walked around amidst the crowds. He'd commandeered her baseball cap and pulled it down low, managing to stay inconspicuous in these much bigger crowds.

Cassie's belly clenched at the low, husky note in his voice. This whole venture had put her libido on high alert. 'But I *like* fireworks,' she said. As a young child Cassie had literally felt transported to the stars amidst all the pop and dazzle.

Tuck grinned. 'Oh, there'll be fireworks. Don't you worry about that.'

Cassie looked at him and could see another night of heaven in his arms. 'Where are we staying tonight?' she asked.

'Ah...' He grinned. 'That's the best bit.' He ducked his head and swiped a mouthful of cotton candy that melted on his tongue. 'Come on—eat that and I'll show you.'

* * *

They drove out of Flagstaff with the Cadillac's top down and headed towards the crater again. A lot of women would have been impressed by the romance, the fifties movie feel—an open-top, a man who could have graced any screen, the open road—but Cassie simply let her head loll back against the headrest and watched the stars float above her.

They passed the road to the crater they'd taken earlier today and some lights could be seen shining from the crater's RV park.

Tuck drove another minute and started to slow. 'I reckon this is as good a spot as any,' he said as he left the road and drove into the desert wilderness, the headlights illuminating an expanse of rocky, arid nothing.

They bumped over some rocks and low vegetation before Tuck turned off the engine and killed the lights, plunging them into the still, inky blackness of a desert night. They hadn't travelled far from the highway and behind them the RV park seemed reasonably close.

'What are you doing?' Cassie asked.

'I want an astronomy lesson,' he said. 'And it just so happens that I'm sleeping with a world-class astronomer. I thought a night under the stars would be kind of cool.'

Cassie looked up again. Millions of stars winked down at her through the obsidian dome of the night sky. It had been so long since she'd looked at them—really looked at them—with the *human eye*. She'd been studying the cosmos for over a decade, and with the advantage of deep-space telescopes and the miracles of modern imaging it was easy to forget the sense of wonder and insignificance she'd used to feel when looking up.

It crowded in on her now, and she took a deep unsteady breath.

'I have luxury bedding in the trunk,' Tuck said. 'I thought we could sleep on the hood of the Caddy.'

Cassie, her head resting back against the leather headrest, rolled her head to the side. It was dark, the one-quarter moon still low in the sky, but she could see Tuck's eyes shining with the same sort of wonder that Marnie's used to hold when she'd begged for an impromptu astronomy session.

'Unless you'd rather check into a hotel?'

Cassie slowly shook her head. It was an ideal night for some star-gazing. 'I can't think of any place more perfect than this,' she murmured. 'Or anyone I'd rather be with.'

Cassie blinked as the words slipped from her lips. Obviously her libido was mouthy, but even she could recognise how the words resonated with her on a much deeper level. She'd found something with Tuck that it had never occurred to her to seek out. And she liked it.

Tuck was taken aback by the spontaneous declaration, and the sincerity in Cassie's gaze. It had been a novelty, being with a woman who didn't cling and wasn't emotionally needy, but it wasn't until this moment that he realised it was also nice to hear her acknowledge that whatever it was they had, she was into it too.

To acknowledge that maybe she needed him as much as he was growing to need her.

'I'll get the stuff,' he said. Because, frankly, he didn't know what to say to such utter honesty. He was so used to *the game* he didn't know how to react when someone played it straight.

Cassie nodded as Tuck climbed out of the car. Another woman might have been puzzled about Tuck's non-re-action to her statement, but Cassie was as eager as Tuck to get flat on her back. And mind-games just weren't her forte.

As it turned out they didn't end up flat on their backs. Tuck adjusted a double sleeping bag with a thick foam mattress on the hood, but when they got inside he propped his back against the windshield and she nestled between his legs, her back to his front, her head on his shoulder, with the entire Arizonan sky stretched like a sheath of black satin above them.

'Do you suppose we'll see a shooting star?' Tuck asked.

His breath stirred the hair at her temple and Cassie momentarily shut her eyes. 'Absolutely,' she said, her eye-lids opening. 'If we watch long enough. Although statis-tically we are more likely to see one after midnight. But you know they're not technically stars, right? They're meteors.'

Tuck lay back and listened to Cassie chatter about a subject on which she obviously knew a great deal. He liked listening to her, and her Australian accent, so ob-vious most of the time, became less distinct as her voice took on a generic wonder.

She pointed out all the constellations, including Cas-siopeia, and was full of facts and figures and interesting anecdotes. The night was perfect, their location even more so, and they did indeed see several shooting stars

over the two hours they sat with their faces turned upwards.

'I suppose you've known all this since you could talk?'
Tuck murmured as she regaled him with some ancient
Greek myths about the constellations.

Cassie nodded. 'I used to spend hours under the stars
with Mum as a little girl. I used to complain about going
to bed and wish we had a glass roof, so I could sleep
under the stars. Then she bought me these glow-in-the-
dark star stickers for my ceiling. There were planets as
well. We mapped the whole solar system out—all geo-
graphically correct, with the constellations accurately
represented—and I got to sleep under the stars every
night.'

Tuck stroked his fingers up and down Cassie's arm.
The desert night air was getting cool now, and he felt
gooseflesh beneath the pads of his fingers. 'You sound
like you're close to your mother?' he said as he pulled
the bedding up around them.

Cassie shrugged. Her relationship with her mother
had always been hard to define. 'Yes and no.'

Tuck heard the wistfulness in her voice. 'Oh?'

Cassie didn't know how to explain it. 'I was the child
that interrupted her astronomy career. Put a stop to
her grand plans of a great discovery that would forever
change the world and a subsequent Nobel Prize. Don't
get me wrong, I fully understand, and she pushed me
to go on and do what she hadn't been able to, but...I
don't know... I think there's part of her that has always
resented the intrusion of a child...of *me*. She loved having me around to teach me things about the stars, but

outside of that there's just this part of her that I never seem to be able to reach...like the stars, I guess.'

Cassie wasn't sure where the calm insights had come from. She'd never given them voice before. Never thought about them too much. But there was a whole lot going on with her emotionally lately that she'd never thought possible. And somehow, cocooned in this warm dark night with Tuck, it seemed right to talk about it.

'What about your dad?' Tuck asked.

'He adores her...but he's never really understood her. Her brilliance. And certainly not why she chose him. He sure as hell doesn't get *me*. So he does his thing, and she does hers, and I do mine and we all live in a kind of oblivious co-existence. I don't know...it works, but I don't think they're happy.'

Tuck thought about the fiery, passionate relationship of his own parents and couldn't even begin to imagine them just *co-existing*. He thought about how passionate his relationship with Cassie was, and the vibrancy of their in-between times too.

Their conversations.

He knew he would never survive in a relationship where everyone *co-existed* and nobody lived.

Cassie shifted against him and heat traced through his groin with all the urgency of a meteor shower. 'Well, I guess it takes all types, honey,' he said as he let his hand drift from her arm to her side, under her shirt and up her ribs to the smooth rise of breast.

Cassie shut her eyes and moaned as his thumb taunted the stiffening peak of her nipple. The stars were forgotten as her nose brushed against his neck, inhaling a mega-dose of pheromones and suddenly her desires went from cosmic to carnal.

She turned in his arms, crawling up his body until she was straddling him. His erection nudged the apex of her thighs and she ground down a little. The harsh suck of his breath was loud in the eerie Arizonian desert and when she lowered her mouth to his their passion ignited.

Before she could blink her shirt was up and off her head and her breasts were bared to the cool night air and to him, and they were kissing and pulling at each other's clothes, and then he was inside her and they were making out on the hood of the car, oblivious to their exposure, driven by the intangible force of nature all around them and their own innate drive to be one.

And Cassie did indeed see fireworks as she came, hard and fast, her head thrown back, her gaze open wide to the stars as they blended in a kaleidoscope of colour and came showering down around her.

NINE

_____

IT FELT LIKE hours later that Cassie stirred from her post-coital doze, but it was probably less than thirty minutes. The cool air was caressing her exposed skin and she needed to take her medication.

'Where are you going?' Tuck murmured as her warmth left his side. He reached for her as she sat up and tugged on her T-shirt.

'Just taking my tablet,' she said as she shrugged into the warmth of the fabric and eased down off the side of the car.

She delved into her handbag, located on the passenger seat. Cold air nipped at her bare legs and crept icy fingers beneath her hem and onto her naked butt as she opened the internal zipper where she'd placed her tablets that morning. She pushed out a small blue pill into her palm and washed it down using the bottle of water that Tuck had bought at Barringer.

She hurried back to Tuck and his big warm body, spread on the hood so invitingly. She dived in beside him and sighed as he gathered her into his chest and pulled the covers up over them.

'I wouldn't have thought you'd need that to sleep any more,' he said, kissing the top of her head. Her hair was cold against his face. 'I thought *I* was your drug of choice?'

Cassie smiled. 'You are. But I still need the other one.'

Tuck stroked his fingers up and down her arm as he gazed absently at the stars. 'Sounds like addiction to me.' He tsked, his voice low, teasing. 'You might have to go cold turkey.'

Cassie tensed against him. *She needed it.* Going off it just wasn't an option.

'I know just the thing you can use as a substitute,' he murmured, his hand stroking lower, moving onto her naked hip.

Cassie didn't even feel the light brush of his fingers as her brain vehemently rejected his suggestion. She pushed herself away, coming up onto her elbow. 'No. I can never go off them. *Never.*'

Tuck blinked at her. Her face was scrunched into a fierce frown, the stars behind her forming a crown. 'O...kay...'

'I *need* them. They keep my brain from racing. They shut it down so I can sleep.'

He grinned again, picking up a lock of hair that had escaped her scrunchie and fallen forward over a bare shoulder. 'That's exactly what an orgasm does. Best sleeping pill there is.'

Cassie sat, pulling her knees up, tucking them against her chest. 'I mean it. The pills and I are a package deal.

I learned the hard way a long time ago that my sanity depends on them.'

Tuck paused. Cassie was rocking slightly, and she looked all wild-eyed beneath the moonlight. 'Hey,' he said, dragging himself up into a sitting position too, 'it's okay. I was just teasing.'

'It's not funny.'

Tuck put his arm around Cassie's shoulders and felt her resist for a moment or two before relaxing against him. He could feel a slight tremble running through her and he didn't think it was from the cold. 'What happened?' he asked, his palm running up and down her arm, warming her.

Cassie didn't say anything for a while. She hadn't really told anyone about that time in any detail. Not because it was a secret, but because she hadn't been close enough to anyone to share it. Apart from that reference to it at the breakfast table at the Bellington Estate, she hadn't even told her college girlfriends.

'I was fourteen. I wasn't a typical teenager. I never really slept a lot—my brain was always busy—but I became convinced there was an error in a textbook that I'd been studying. I became obsessed with it—up all night on the computer trying to cross-reference, e-mailing hundreds of experts in the field trying to prove I was right, e-mailing the publishers, constantly harassing them to have it fixed. My brain was full of it. My schoolwork was ignored and I couldn't sleep. I was surviving on less and less each night until I wasn't even getting an hour's respite.'

Cassie stopped. With the benefit of time and clearer

thought-processes she could see how trivial it had been, and how fanatical and irrational she'd become, but it had felt like a matter of national importance at the time.

'It was all I talked about, all I thought about. I barely ate. I couldn't sit still long enough to eat. Eventually I was admitted to hospital with dehydration. But I was rambling about it...*raving*, I suppose is a better word. And from there I was admitted to a psych unit.'

Tuck's hold on her tightened as her voice, husky in the silence of the night, gave away the turmoil not evidenced in her dispassionate words. He guessed this kind of thing was the flipside of genius.

'They drugged me up. I lost days...weeks...where I was this zombie. Where I had no say or control over my life. I couldn't think. My mind was blank. I could barely feed myself.' She shuddered. 'Eventually they got my medication right and I came out of the fog. It was scary.' She looked at him. 'And I never want to go there again.'

'Shh,' Tuck said, kissing her forehead, amazed at what she'd been through. At how susceptible her genius had made her. 'I understand. The medication gives you control.'

Cassie nodded. 'More than anything, I learned that my brain needs sleep to be healthy, to perform at its highest level. *To be me.* And if that means I have to swallow one little pill every night for the rest of my life, even if I have to wake up to do it, then that's what I'm going to do. Because the alternative...'

Tuck felt her shudder again and pulled her harder against him, wrapping both his arms around her shoulders. This was the first time he'd ever seen her vulnerable and he couldn't help but feel that they'd taken a major step forward.

'Is unacceptable,' he finished for her. 'I know,' he agreed. 'I know.'

The distant rumble of an engine from the direction of the RV park woke Cassie at six the next morning. She was snuggled into Tuck's side, her head on his shoulder, all warm and cosy despite the cool air on her face. She stretched and rolled on her back. The inky obsidian of last night had morphed into a crystal-clear desert dawn, with a slight blush of pink tingeing the pale blue arc that stretched endlessly to the distant horizon.

She smiled as Tuck rolled towards her, his big arm clamping around her waist, his lips nuzzling her neck.

'We have to get going,' he murmured into her hair, reluctant as all hell to leave their deliciously warm cocoon. He felt closer to her this morning after her revelation last night than he'd ever felt. But they had a Gulf Stream to catch. 'The plane leaves in an hour.'

Cassie nodded. Ordinarily she would have sprung up and been keen to get back home. To Cornell. She was essentially losing two days out of her academic schedule by taking this time out. But she wouldn't have missed this in a million years. Being here, seeing Barringer, having a truly magical night under the stars…

And all because of Tuck.

Lying here, in his arms, she was grateful that she'd have this amazing memory to take back home with her. But more than that she was beginning to think that maybe there might be more to life than twenty-four-seven study.

And, surprisingly, it *didn't* scare the hell out of her.

A minute later Tuck kissed her neck. 'Come on—time to shake a tail feather.' And he hauled himself up into a sitting position.

'I don't know where my clothes are.' Cassie yawned. She'd lost her shirt again not long after her confession to him last night.

Tuck threw back the covers and looked down at her naked body, stretched before him. It had a predictable effect on him and his body snapped to instant awareness.

'Clothes are overrated,' he said as he trailed a hand down her body from the hollow of her throat to her pubic bone. He eased himself back on his elbow, leaned in and kissed her neck, his hand easing back up her body to cup a breast.

Cassie shivered as the cool morning breeze sizzled across her heated skin. She stretched her neck to give him better access, and when his hand travelled south again and slipped between her legs they opened eagerly. When the pad of his thumb stroked against her centre she moaned. When one finger probed, then slipped inside, she arched her back. When another joined it she called his name. And when his head followed the path of his hands and settled between her legs Cassie surrendered to the maelstrom.

She built quickly, the speed and strength of her orgasm multiplying as visual data from all around bombarded her senses. The perfect arc of blue sky, the vast flatness rolling all the way out to the horizon, the eerie quiet broken only by her delirious cries, the cool breeze, and Tuck's blond head between her legs doing that thing he did that pushed her over the edge *every single time*.

The overpowering visuals coalesced and ripples of release fanned through her belly. She lifted her hips as they became hard and unrelenting. She cried out, jack-knifing up as they flung her into space and her whole world threatened to collapse in on her. She thrust her hand into his hair, holding him fast, riding the wave and the hard edge of his tongue until her body shattered and fell and twirled back to earth. She collapsed back against the hood, shamelessly spread before him and the sky above like some pagan sacrifice, overwhelmingly sated.

Another engine noise caused her to stir a little while later and she opened her eyes. Tuck was kissing his way back up her body. 'We really *do* have to go,' he said against her neck as he dropped her shirt on her belly.

Cassie was fairly incapable of speech. She could see the highway not far away, and the first RV of the day turning on to it, heading in their direction.

Tuck lay down beside her, lifting his hips as he eased his shorts up. 'I think I'll need to investigate the bottom of the sleeping bag a little more thoroughly to find the rest of our clothes,' he said.

The RV pulled to the side of the road, in their direct line of sight, but still probably a hundred or so metres from them. Tuck looked up, frowning at the intrusion into their private little bubble.

'Come on then, Cassiopeia,' he said as he heard a car door open and close. 'If these people are stopping to ask us if we're okay we'd better be dressed.' He swung his legs off the hood and jumped to the ground. 'Of course...' his gaze fanned over her again '...if you just want to stay here for ever like that with me then I'm sure I could arrange that too.'

Cassie shook herself out of her post-coital daze at Tuck's reminder that there was a world for them to get back to. That Cornell was waiting. She pulled her shirt over her head and Tuck held out his hand to help her down.

The wind caught her shirt and it billowed out as Tuck lifted her down. Cassie felt the breeze cool places that were still quite overheated, but was thankful that she favoured baggy shirts—she didn't fancy giving the man at the side of the road an eyeful, no matter how distant.

She stumbled against Tuck as her feet hit the dirt and one of them found a sharp little rock. 'Ow!' She cursed, screwing up her face at the jab of pain.

'You okay?' Tuck asked, grabbing her by the arms to steady her.

Cassie nodded as she breathed through the pain. 'Fine,' she said on a sucked-in breath.

Tuck grinned down at her. 'You're kind of cute when you cuss.'

She glared at him, but his hand was sliding onto her jaw and his mouth was descending and his kiss swept the indignation, the pain and every IQ point she owned into the ether. His pheromones filled her head and Cassie clung to his naked chest as they made her dizzy.

Tuck pulled away, groaning against her mouth. 'We *have* to go.'

A minute later the RV left, and ten minutes after

that they were on the road back to Flagstaff. Within the hour they were wheels up and winging their way back to Ithica.

Two nights later Cassie shut the lid of her laptop around ten. Tuck was sitting up in bed, his long, muscular legs crossed at the ankles, watching a Thursday night game on the massive big screen television that dominated the wall opposite their bed. He had the sound turned down low for her benefit, but he really needn't have bothered. Cassie easily became consumed in her work to the exclusion of everything else. The street could have exploded and she'd have been oblivious.

He gave her a goofy grin, one of several he'd given her since she'd come home, and she frowned. He'd been mysterious about his day too. 'You're up to something,' she said.

Tuck feigned a hurt look. 'Not me.'

Cassie smiled at his obvious lie. 'I'm having a shower.'

'I'll be here waiting for you when you get back,' he said.

Cassie eyed him suspiciously as she headed for the bathroom. She was tired. *Good* tired. Ready to go to sleep tired. She'd never felt tired prior to meeting Tuck. She'd always been a little on the wired side and her need for that one little pill had never been questioned. But Tuck was right. Sexual satisfaction was a powerful sedative— a pity they couldn't bottle it.

Cassie was in and out of the shower in ten minutes, padding back into the room in just her underwear, her hair in its regulation ponytail. She could feel his eyes leave the television and follow her every movement as she went through the drawers searching for a shirt.

'You shouldn't bother with a shirt,' Tuck said, eyeing the swing of her breasts, football game forgotten.

Cassie turned to face him, her nipples responding to the blatant strain of sex in his voice. 'Oh?'

Tuck laughed at the slogan on her underwear. It had a Pi sign and read 'I speak geek'. He held out his hand. 'Come to bed *just* like that.'

Tuck was wearing a pair of boxer briefs and nothing else and Cassie was drawn across the room, his voice wrapping silky strands around her waist and slowly tugging. She detoured around to her side of the bed and peeled the sheet back as she climbed in. Tuck flicked the TV off with the remote and Cassie reached out to snap off the lights, plunging the room into darkness.

Except there wasn't complete darkness. An eerie green glow lit the ceiling and Cassie gasped as she looked up and saw hundreds of glow-in-the-dark stars covering the huge expanse of ceiling in the very large room.

She looked at Tuck. 'You did this today?'

He nodded. 'I paid one of the astronomy majors to do me an exact replica of our solar system. You like?'

Cassie squirmed down until she was lying on her back. 'Cassiopeia,' she said, pointing to the constellation as familiar to her as her own name.

Tuck lay down beside her and they star-gazed as they had that other night in Arizona, except indoors this time.

'Are you even allowed to do this?' she asked, glancing

at him as they exhausted the solar system. 'Defacing a rental apartment?'

Tuck shrugged. 'I'll pay to have them removed and the ceiling returned to all its boring plainness if they want when we're done here.'

'Yes, it *was* kind of boring, wasn't it?' she murmured as the stars glowed down at her. 'But not any more.'

Tuck nodded. Just like his life. It had been boring and predictable before Cassie. He knew that sounded ungrateful, that plenty of people had lives that were barely tolerable and that his life had been very good. There'd been many years when he'd enjoyed it and the perks that came with it. But being on the celebrity treadmill, going through the motions, was about as appealing now as a plain white ceiling.

If he wasn't careful he'd forget that they had an expiry date.

'And the best part is,' Tuck said, rolling up onto his elbow, looking down at her, 'I literally get to make you see stars every night.'

Cassie shut her eyes as his scent wafted over her and breathed him deep into her lungs. The primal urge to feel him inside her bloomed deep and low.

'But I think it's only fair that you get to see them first.' She pushed on his chest. When he fell back against the bed she rolled on top of him.

Tuck smiled up at her as she straddled him, naked but for her underwear, just like that night in the desert. 'Okay...' he said, his palms sliding up her torso, finding her breasts. 'If you insist.'

But his hands soon fell away as her intent became

clear, and when she kissed her way down his body and right into his boxer briefs he felt as if he'd snatched a little piece of heaven from off the ceiling.

The next morning the bubble they'd been living in, tucked away in Ithica, away from the rest of the world, well and truly burst. It was a phone call from Marnie that alerted Cassie to the looming disaster.

'How you doin', hon? Are you okay?' Marnie asked.

Cassie stopped looking at the data on her computer screen and frowned. There was something in Marnie's Southern twang that put her on high alert. 'Er...yes... sure... Why wouldn't I be?'

'Oh. You haven't seen it, then?' she asked.

'Seen what?'

'The tabloid article?'

Cassie went back to her work. 'About the paternity stuff? That's old news.'

'No, not that. Same tabloid but...it's about *you* and Tuck. There's some not very flattering pics, and the headline...it's pretty awful.'

It was sweet of Marnie to alert her, but Cassie just didn't care about celebrity gossip or the weird obsession people had with it. 'I'm sure I'll survive,' she said dryly.

'Okay...just don't... Ignore it, okay? Anyone who knows you knows how beautiful you are—inside and out.'

Cassie frowned at the odd parting remark, but was quickly absorbed in her work again.

Gina phoned next, followed by Reese. She assured both of them that she was fine and had better things to jumping on as many heads as he possibly could before she got home.

'You've *seen* it?'

'No,' she said. 'But I've had phone calls from Reese, Gina and Marnie about it.'

Damn! He hadn't thought about them. 'It's okay. By the time I'm through with them they'll think the Jenny debacle was a freaking Sunday school picnic.'

Cassie stepped out of his arms. This seemed a lot of fuss about some dumb tabloid article. 'For goodness' sake, what does it say?'

'Oh. They didn't tell you?'

'No, I was busy doing *important* things, like my PhD research at the very place where *Carl Sagan* himself studied. Now, what the hell does it say that has everyone in such a tizz? Have you got a copy?'

Tuck looked behind him at the pile of newspapers he'd bought from practically every newsstand in Ithica. 'One or two,' he said.

Cassie blinked at the stacks that littered the formal dining table and the nearby floor. She marched over, picked one off the top and opened it. The glaring headline on page three jumped out at her—*'Tuck's Ugly Duck'*.

There were several pictures. One was of them at Barringer Crater, where she looked all hot and bedraggled, and three more had been taken the next morning. One was a shot of the wind billowing under her T-shirt, so she looked like the Michelin man, another was of her face all screwed up when that rock had jabbed into her, and the last was their passionate kiss just after that, with Tuck all bare-chested.

do with her time than worry about tabloid gossip. And she put it out of her mind.

Until she arrived home at seven and Tuck was pacing in front of the large windows, yelling into his phone.

'I don't just want an apology. I want a price put on that pap's head. I want him dead or alive. I want the whole freaking paper shut down. I want to tie them up in the world's most expensive legal case until they're haemorrhaging money. They think they can mess with me after the Jenny thing? They just made me their worst freaking enemy!'

Cassie jumped as Tuck hurled his phone at the glass. It bounced off and crashed to the ground. He raked a hand through his hair, ignoring the felled piece of expensive technology.

'Hi,' she said.

Tuck turned and saw her standing there. He took half a dozen long strides and swept her into his arms. He didn't say anything, but she could tell from the fierceness of his hug that he was still angry.

Tuck pulled back and looked into Cassie's blue-grey eyes. They'd become such a part of his life he couldn't begin to imagine a time when she wouldn't be here, all calm and thoughtful. And that made him even crazier—their time together was definitely finite!

'There's something I have to tell you,' he said.

'Is this about the tabloid article?' she asked.

Tuck gaped. When his PA had first alerted him that morning he hadn't thought that Cassie would want her day interrupted—plus he hadn't wanted to tell her over the phone. So he'd left informing her in preference to

They were a little fuzzy, but it was definitely them.

The article speculated as to who she was and how un-like Tuck's usual glamorous consorts she was. It seemed to be drawing a parallel between the fading of his star and his luck in the lady stakes. Cassie rolled her eyes and threw the paper down in disgust.

'It was that bastard in the RV,' Tuck said, resuming his pacing. 'He has to have been paparazzi too—not just some visitor wanting to cash in on an unexpected opportunity. You'd need a serious camera to get those images of us.'

Cassie thought about it for a moment. 'It was the guy with the big gold jewellery,' she said.

Tuck stopped pacing. 'What? Why didn't you tell me there was a pap around?'

She shrugged. 'I didn't realise he was at the time.'

'Well, what makes you think it was him now?'

'He kind of hung around a bit. He asked me if you were my boyfriend. He commented that I wasn't your usual type. He looked kind of puzzled as to why we were together. He had a little boy with him...Zack...you signed an autograph for him.'

Tuck nodded. He remembered. The man hadn't been familiar—and Tuck had got to know most of the paps over the years.

'Good,' he said, stalking over and picking his phone up off the floor. He hit the last call button.

Cassie listened to the one-sided conversation as Tuck relayed the details to his lawyer and they discussed ways to access Barringer Crater's records of who had come through that day. Tuck paced again as he spoke, and even though his anger seemed less palpable she could sense frustration surging off him in waves, much the same way she'd always been sensitive to his pheromones.

Tuck hung up the phone and turned to face Cassie. 'I'm sorry. I'm so, so sorry,' he said, trying to gauge how Cassie was feeling about the article. 'I won't let them get away with this.'

Cassie shrugged. 'Get away with what? Who cares what they think?'

Tuck blinked. Any other woman he knew would be *outraged* at that headline. 'But they've insulted you,' he said.

Cassie snorted. 'You think I'm *insulted*? You think how *beautiful* you are counts when you're up for a Nobel Prize? Those things don't go to the *prettiest* candidate, Tuck. You think *science* cares about what you look like? You think they select people to go to Antarctica based on their *attractiveness*? I really don't think you realise how very, very little this matters to me.'

'They don't have the right to say such horribly hurtful things in a national newspaper about you,' Tuck said, his anger once again exploding to the surface at Cassie's calm acceptance. 'About *any* woman.' Didn't she realise how beautiful she was?

Cassie shook her head, amazed at how angry he seemed to be. But then she supposed it *was* a bit of a slap in the face for Tuck, who was used to accolades, to being known for his beautiful women.

'Oh...I see,' she said. 'This isn't about *me*. This is about an affront to your *masculinity*. That some two-bit rag has the *audacity* to call one of *your* women ugly. Are you afraid you're not going to make the A-list any more with an ugly, brainiac *girlfriend*?' She shook her head. 'Just what the hell are you doing with me, Tuck?'

Tuck couldn't believe the words that were coming out of her mouth. Rage, white and hot, built in his gut and leeched into his bloodstream. How could she think he was so damn shallow?

'I don't *care* about that crap,' he snapped, shoving his hands on his hips. 'But I *do* care when a national newspaper calls *any* woman ugly. Who has the right to be the arbiter of that? The right to say it? And you? You are smart and sexy and warm and intelligent and beautiful and *natural* in a way beyond anything any of those *twits* with their freaking airbrushes and computer programs would know anything about, and I'm not going to sit still and let them call one of the most brilliant minds on the planet, *and the woman I love*, ugly.'

Tuck was breathing hard when he finished. In fact it took him a few seconds before he even realised what he'd said.

'What did you say?' Cassie said.

He'd said he loved her. His first instinct was to take it back. Pretend that it had been said in the heat of the moment and not meant. But, whilst it had *totally* been said in the heat of the moment, he did mean it. *He loved her.* He just hadn't realised it 'til that moment.

He'd almost spat his coffee all over the paper this morning when he'd first read the article, and his anger had been building with the ominous power and thrust of a dangerous weather front all day. He hadn't been able to articulate where the immediate irrational anger had come from when he'd first dialled his lawyer, but it had been frighteningly, utterly palpable.

And now he knew why.

He'd never felt like this about a woman. Not even April. He'd wanted to love her like this, had committed to that, but the plain truth was that he'd only ever just liked her, and she'd been there to cling to when everything was spiralling down the plughole. But it hadn't been enough, and he'd been wrong to give her hope that he could love her as she'd deserved.

As he *loved* Cassie.

'I love you,' he said. And then he said it again for good measure, weighing it up. 'I love you.'

He'd spent a lot of his life thinking those three words would mean his life was over, but it didn't feel like that— it felt as if it was just beginning. It wasn't scary and awful—it was just *right*.

Cassie blinked. 'Don't be ridiculous,' she said. 'Even if I believed that such an emotion existed, and wasn't some commercial construct to sell movies and Valentines, we've known each other for just over a month— it's preposterous.'

Tuck shook his head. 'It's not.'

Cassie couldn't believe what she was hearing. Len might never have performed oral sex on her and blown her head right off her shoulders every single night, but he would never have complicated their arrangement by falling prey to such schoolboy fancy. This was what happened when she got involved with someone who let his heart—or other parts of his body—rule his head.

Now she understood why her mother had been so

determined to school her in the importance of her career and not to let distractions derail her from what was truly important.

Declarations like this could stop a person in their tracks!

But not her. She had her PhD to finish, then she was heading home to Australia, and next year she was going to Antarctica—come hell or high water. And she was *not* going to let some jock talk her out of it because he *imagined* himself in love with her.

Love was for dreamers—not thinkers. And she was most definitely a thinker.

It just wasn't *logical* that he loved her, for crying out loud!

'Well, I don't love you,' she said.

Tuck flinched at her matter-of-fact delivery. 'You're telling me you don't feel *anything* for me?'

Cassie shrugged. 'I feel sexual arousal. I feel a Pavlovian response to your pheromones. I feel a constant state of primal awareness.'

'Well, that's a start,' he said.

'I'm here because of my libido, Tuck. That's why you invited me, remember? It was never about anything other than burning off some lust.' Even as she said the words she knew they weren't one hundred percent true. 'We always had an end date.'

Tuck took a step towards her. He'd thought they'd grown closer over the last weeks, that Cassie had started to see their relationship as something more than a scratching post for her libido. Especially since their time at Barringer—since she'd told him about what had happened to her as a teenager.

'What if I don't want that any more? What if I want more?'

'*More?*'

'A relationship. Marriage. A family.'

It was Cassie's turn to gape. Since when had Mr-Love-Them-and-Leave-Them got so serious? Hadn't he said her complete lack of interest in weddings and babies was right up his alley?

'In a couple of months I'm going home to *Australia,* to continue my aurora research, and next year I'm going to *Antarctica* for six months. I'm not going to have *any* regrets in my life, Tuck. Not like my mother. I don't believe in love and marriage. And children aren't on my agenda. You know that.'

Tuck could feel it all slipping away. 'A career and a family don't have to be mutually exclusive.'

'You can't even *have* children, Tuck.' She saw him flinch at her blunt statement and felt conflicted by how bad it felt. *Damn it—it was the truth.* 'I didn't think you *wanted* them.'

Tuck hadn't. Not really. Not even when he'd been going through the fertility process with April. But *she* had, and it had seemed like something to bond them together even though his infertility had exacerbated his already battered sense of self.

'I do now,' he said, realising the truth of it. 'I want to have children with you.'

Cassie shook her head. 'I'll be gone for *six months,* Tuck. And it won't be the only time my career will have me travelling. You'd be okay with that, would you?'

Tuck blanched at the thought. He missed her like

crazy during her twelve-hour days at the university. Six months would seem like an eternity.

Cassie nodded at his hesitation. 'Clearly this is not working. I'll move back to the dorm.'

She headed for the bedroom. She should be calm. It was, after all, a logical decision to move on now things were not as she'd originally agreed. But her heart was thumping and there was an ache in the pit of her stomach as if she was ravenously hungry but there was nothing she wanted to eat.

Tuck took some deep breaths before he followed her in. His heart thundered and his head spun at how everything had unravelled so quickly. Cassie was throwing her clothes into her case when he joined her.

'Don't do this,' he said from the doorway.

Cassie shook her head. 'It's logical,' she said, not looking at him. 'I moved in because it was logical and now—given the way that we both feel—it's logical for me to move out.'

Tuck didn't know what he'd expected. Women he'd split with before had never been this calm. There'd been tears. Anger. Threats. It should have made a nice change, but it only made it virtually impossible to reach her. She'd reverted to her comfort zone of logic and sense and that was as far removed from gut and emotion as was possible.

He was angry and frustrated, but it seemed futile in the midst of her calm, detached packing. How could he get through to a robot? It was ironic that when he'd finally fallen in love with a woman it was with one who was incapable of returning it.

His Great-Aunt Ada would have said it was poetic justice.

'Don't,' he snapped, moving into the room. 'Stay. I'll move. I'll go back to New York. Stay until you're done here. It's paid up for three months.'

'Don't be ridiculous,' Cassie said, automatically concentrating very hard on the job at hand instead of the growing gnaw in her gut. 'This is your place.'

Tuck reached over and slammed the drawer shut. 'I said don't,' he barked. 'You want logic? A dorm is no place for a grown woman. It makes *sense* for you stay here. Put some of those IQ points of yours to good use and *figure it out.*'

Cassie couldn't look at him as he loomed over her. His pheromones wafted off him in strong waves and despite the situation her nostrils flared. If he didn't go soon she was going to act in a very confusing and contradictory manner.

For both of them.

'Okay. Thank you,' she said.

Tuck nodded. He went to the bedside table and picked up his wallet and keys. 'I'll send for my stuff tomorrow.'

Cassie didn't acknowledge him. She didn't turn to watch him leave. She just stood by the drawers and listened to the door slam, the car start up, the garage door open, the car drive away.

And, despite knowing logically it was better this way, the pain in her gut grew bigger.

TEN

———

BAD NEWS TRAVELLED fast, and Cassie spent the next week taking phone calls from her concerned friends, assuring them that she was fine, that it was for the best. That she and Tuck had only ever been a temporary sexual thing and he'd got too emotionally involved.

And she believed it. In her head.

But the gnawing pain just didn't seem to go away, no matter how much she ate. On top of that a heaviness had taken up residence in her chest. And once again her work was shot. But this time it wasn't about her libido or her hormones, which was the most confusing thing— because even though she'd never really understood that at least she was familiar with it.

This was about something else entirely. It was about *him*. She couldn't stop thinking about *him*. Memories of their time together interrupted her days and bombarded her dreams.

Their Sunday mornings together reading the papers. Sharing an evening meal and talking about their day.

Their quiet companionship every night as they worked on their projects, her at the desk in the bedroom, Tuck propped against the bedhead, a game turned on low.

And the trip to Barringer. The mystery plane ride, the open-top Cadillac, exploring the crater with him, eating candy floss, their night of stargazing, opening up to him.

And the hot, wild sex under a desert night.

Yes, okay, some of her thoughts *did* linger on their crazy, insatiable sex-life. Because she did miss the sex too. But she'd always figured that the sex would be the thing she'd miss *the most* when their relationship ended.

But it wasn't. *She missed him.* She missed him being around. Being right there. Filling up the spaces in the kitchen, the bathroom, the bedroom. Filling up the silences. She missed turning around to talk to him, to show him some miraculous cosmic image, to talk about the intricacies of her project, to ask him about his.

She hadn't realised how silent her life had been until Tuck had been there, filling it up with light and sound and noise.

It wasn't logical to feel this way. She *never* had before. It didn't make sense.

But it wouldn't go away either.

And then the weekend swung around and it was all that Cassie could do to drag herself out of bed on Saturday. She hadn't been sleeping well, despite the medication, and when she did she dreamt of Tuck. It didn't seem to matter what she did, what drug she took, how hard she worked or how late she stayed up to thoroughly exhaust herself, she couldn't switch her brain off from thinking about him.

The last thing she felt like doing was hitting the re-search—and she *always* felt like hitting the research. She knew it would be a distraction from her thoughts, something to help get her through another long day, but when she got there a whole batch of new images had come in overnight and she found herself thinking about Tuck even more. One of them was an ultraviolet image of a star cluster on the edge of the solar system, and it reminded her of the blue of Tuck's eyes so much she lost her breath.

She itched to ring him. To tell him about the majesty and beauty of the pictures. He'd been as fascinated by the images on her laptop as she had, and this image more than any other seemed to resonate with her.

It was like staring straight into his blue, blue gaze.

Damn it.

At three o'clock Cassie gave up trying to be produc-tive and headed for home. The next six weeks stretched ahead interminably, and she hated that what should have been the highlight of her life had completely lost its lustre. She would forever look back on it and think not of her exciting time in one of the great cradles of learning but of Tuck.

The only consolation, as she put one foot in front of the other, was that she got to go back to the apartment instead of the dorm. At least she could be miserable in solitude.

When she got in she stripped off her leggings and fell into bed. Utter exhaustion finally took over and, as her head hit the pillow, she fell headlong into a dark and troubled sleep. Elusive images of Tuck and her mother intertwined with deep-space images so they seemed to float in a galaxy of stars, and every time she reached out to touch him, to touch her mother, they disappeared in her hand like rainbow mist.

It took the simultaneous beating on her door and the ringing of her mobile phone a few hours later to yank her out of the increasingly distressing dream. She woke with a start, her heart pounding, disorientated for a few moments. Then the noises started to filter in and she leapt from the bed, heading for the door, collecting her ringing phone on the way and answering it.

'Hello?' she said as she walked.

'It's us!' A chorus of voices reverberated through her ear.

'We're at your door,' Reese said.

'Let us in,' Gina demanded.

Cassie faltered for a moment as she neared the door, then hurried to open it, the phone still pressed to her ear.

A cheer of, 'Surprise!' and a cacophony of party horns greeted her. Cassie hit the 'end' button on her phone just in time as her *gal pals* descended upon her, pulling her into a group hug.

'We've come to get you drunk,' Gina said, waving two bottles of champagne in the air.

Marnie, her perky blonde ponytail swinging, frowned at Gina. 'We've come to *cheer you up,*' she clarified, and Cassie guessed things were still a little cool between the two women.

'How are you, hon?' Reese said, hugging her hard again. 'My cousin's obviously been hit too many times in the head.' She pulled back. 'I could probably get Mason to send around some of his Marine buddies and rough him up a little, if you like?'

Cassie was temporarily speechless. She'd been struggling along for over a week now, pretending she was okay, but just having her oldest friends here made her feel as if she actually *was* going to be okay. That she was going to be able to survive this thing she didn't even understand.

It had never occurred to her to call them to her side, but she was so glad they were here. Tears sprang to her eyes. She blinked them away—for Pete's sake, she *never* cried!

'We have movies,' Marnie said, holding up three DVDs that looked distinctly science-fictiony.

'And we're ordering pizza,' Reese added. 'Do you have a local number? I can't believe Tuck wouldn't,' she said, wandering off to investigate the fridge for a magnet or a menu.

Gina looked around and whistled. 'Nice digs. You scored well. Did he leave anything we could trash?'

Cassie shook her head, feeling more tears threaten. 'Everything's gone.'

Gina hugged her. 'It's okay,' she said. 'We'll trash talk about him on social media instead, like all good ex-girl-friends. Now, come on—where are your glasses?'

Cassie was swept up in the noise and light that was the Awesome Foursome and it felt good to be part of them again. To be part of their circle, to feel their love, to know that they'd slay dragons for her.

Or at least contribute to the hire of a hit-man.

And they didn't talk about Tuck—not to start with anyway. They drank champagne and toasted friendship and regaled Cassie with stories of their own recent lives while they waited for the pizza to be delivered. But as they sat at the table to eat the questioning began.

Gina went first. 'You want to talk about it?' she asked in her usual blunt manner.

Cassie didn't know. She'd certainly listened to enough tales of woe and break-up stories from her friends over the year she'd lived with them to know *talking about it* was what you were *supposed* to do. But it really hadn't been a position she'd envisaged herself in.

'Not really.'

'Was it the newspaper article?' Marnie asked, extending her hand and placing it over Cassie's forearm where it lay on the table.

Cassie shook her head. 'I don't care about some stupid headline in some stupid gossip rag.'

'No...I meant the paternity suit,' Marnie said as she gently squeezed Cassie's wrist.

'No.' Cassie withdrew her arm and reached for a slice of pepperoni pizza. 'I don't care about that either. And it's been dropped anyway.'

The women all looked at each other as Cassie bit into her pizza. 'Did he snore?' Marnie asked.

'Drop his wet towels on the floor?' Reese suggested.

'Pick his teeth at the table?' Gina said.

'I know,' Marnie said. 'He was vulgar with his money.'

Reese snorted. 'Hardly. I know... I bet he treated you like some Texan princess—a china doll.'

'Or maybe he was just lousy in bed?' Gina said.

Cassie almost choked on her pizza at the last suggestion, necessitating some back-bashing action from Gina.

Reese pushed Cassie's champagne towards her and said, 'Drink.'

When Cassie had her voice back she said, 'He did none of those things. He had perfect manners with food and his money and was well house-trained. And he most definitely was *not* lousy in bed. The man achieved the impossible with me. *Time and again.*'

Cassie's belly looped the loop at the thought of how many times Tuck had brought her to orgasm.

'Damn, I *knew* he'd be good,' Gina said wistfully.

Marnie shot her a quelling look. 'So what *did* happen?'

Cassie sighed at her well-intentioned friends gazing back at her, wanting to help. Wanting to understand so they could make things better. And who knew? Maybe they could. This was obviously a time when *EQ*, which they all had in spades, trumped IQ, which *she* had in spades but obviously meant *zip*.

'He told me he loved me.'

Marnie looked at her, puzzled. Gina and Reese exchanged an eyebrow-raise. Yep. Definitely an *EQ* thing.

'That's...it?' Reese asked.

'But...that's a good thing, Cass,' Marnie said gently.

Reese nodded. 'Most available women on this continent—hell, most of the unavailable ones too—would kill to hear those words come out of Samuel Tucker's mouth.'

Cassie threw down her half-eaten piece of pizza. 'I'm not most women. I never have been. You all know that.'

They nodded in unison. Truer words had never been spoken.

Cassie downed her champagne in one swallow. 'I don't *fall* in love. I don't *believe* in love. It's the most illogical, irrational...*thing*...in the entire universe. So much time and effort and money is wasted on it. Trying to achieve it, trying to keep it. We'd have a cure for cancer or poverty or a manned flight to Mars by now if people just channelled the same amount of energy into *important* things that they do into something as fanciful as love.'

'No such thing as love?' Marnie blanched. 'I thought you didn't believe in it like you didn't believe in God or unicorns or pots of gold at the ends of rainbows. Not that you *seriously* denied its existence.' She took a sip of her champagne. 'What about the love a mother has for her newborn baby?'

'That's evolution,' Cassie dismissed. 'Mothers are pre-conditioned to love. It hones their protective instincts to keep their offspring alive in the world so they can go on to continue the species. But what purpose is there for romantic love?' Cassie demanded.

'Procreation?' Marnie said.

Cassie shook her head. 'Survival of the species is maintained perfectly well without it in all species except humans.'

'Sometimes not even then,' said Gina, ever the cynic.

'How about just because it feels good?' Reese murmured.

Cassie snorted. 'Lots of things feel good.' Sex with Tuck had felt exceptionally good. 'Doesn't mean it's good *for* us. Feeling good is not a reason to do something.'

Reese blinked. 'Why not?'

'Because then we only do the things we want instead

of the things we *need* to do. It's not conducive to the survival of the fittest.'

The women fell silent at an impasse they didn't seem
to be able to bridge.

'Come on,' Gina said after a moment or two, filling
their glasses again. 'We're not here to be downers. We're
here to cheer you up. Let's go and watch some movies.
We even rented the first three *Star Treks*, just for you.'

Cassie watched as the bubbles in her champagne rose
to the surface. She picked up her glass and raised it towards her friends. 'Thank you for all coming. I know this
touchy-feely stuff isn't my forte, but I'm glad you're here
dishing it out anyway. And I'm touched that you hired
my favourite movies. I know you'd all rather stick yourself in the eye with a hot poker.'

'Cheers to that,' Gina muttered as she clinked her
glass with Cassie's. 'Now, let's get this party started.'

By the time the credits had rolled on the third movie
it was well after midnight, the two bottles of champagne
were gone and they'd emptied two more bottles of wine
Gina had discovered on a wire rack inside the pantry.

'Well, that's eight hours of my life I'm never going
to get back,' Gina said as she stretched out on the bed.

They'd all piled into the king-sized bed to watch the
DVDs on the big screen.

'Feeling better now?' Marnie asked as she glanced
at Cassie.

Cassie nodded. 'Yes. Thank you.' And she did. A night
with her *gal pals* had taken her mind off Tuck. She'd even

laughed through Gina and Reese's alternative running commentary of the movie. 'Thank you for coming.'

She felt as if she'd gained some perspective, having her friends around. There was no need to feel so overwhelmed by things she didn't understand when she had such great women in her life—at the end of a telephone.

'I was feeling sorry for myself. But not any more.'

'You look better,' Marnie said.

'I feel much stronger,' Cassie agreed.

'Good. Our work here is done.' Reese smiled, settling down onto her pillow. 'Now, turn the lights out and let's get some sleep. We've got a long drive back to New York in the morning and none of us are nineteen any more.'

Cassie reached out and flipped off the lights and was greeted by a chorus of gasps. She looked up at hundreds of stars glowing down at her.

'Wow,' Gina said.

'Cassie,' Marnie whispered. 'It's beautiful. Did you do that?'

Cassie felt her eyes fill with tears and the stars grew halos, then they danced and twisted as they refracted through the rapidly building moisture.

'No,' she said, her voice wobbly. 'Tuck did.'

Suddenly the pain in her stomach reached excruciating levels, and then it exploded with such force it took her breath away. A sob rose in her throat and she choked on it as her lungs fought for space inside a chest welling with sensation. Another sob rose, and then another, until she was full-on crying.

So much for feeling stronger.

Reese sat up. 'Cassie?'

The others followed suit. Marnie reached over and flicked the light back on. They stared at their friend, not sure what to do or say. They'd never seen Cassie cry. It had only been tonight they'd seen her in any kind of emotional quandary at all.

'Cassie?' Gina said, hauling Cassie upright and pulling her into a big hug, stroking her hair.

'What's wrong, honey?' Reese murmured, rubbing Cassie's back.

'I don't know what's wrong with me,' Cassie howled into Gina's neck. But it was scaring the hell out of her. This loss of control was eerily similar to that torrid time in her teens, and she was frightened she was losing her mind. 'I don't cry. I *never* cry. I want it to stop.'

'It's okay,' Marnie added. 'You cry all you want. Crying's good. It's natural in this sort of situation. Trust me, I know it's not big in geek land, but sometimes, as a woman, there's nothing that beats a good old-fashioned howl.'

This was natural? Cassie couldn't believe that something so preposterous could be true. But none of her friends was looking at her as if she was going crazy, and nor did she seem to be able to stop.

'Really?' she sobbed.

Everyone nodded, and somehow she felt reassured that this was part and parcel of whatever the hell was happening to her, not a spiral into something deep and dark, so she just kept her head on Gina's shoulder and let every single tear fall free.

Twenty minutes later the tears had settled to some hiccoughy sighs, and Cassie pulled herself off Gina's shoulder. Reese handed her a wad of tissues. 'Thanks,' Cassie said. 'I seriously don't know what's come over me lately.'

'Have you ever thought,' Gina said, approaching the subject gently, 'maybe you love him?'

Reese and Marnie looked at each other, stunned that such a thought had come from Gina, who had declared herself pretty much divorced from the emotion herself.

Cassie shook her head again. 'No. I told you I don't believe in love.'

'Well, sometimes that doesn't really matter,' Reese said, jumping in. God knew, she'd been whammied by love at a most inconvenient time. 'Some of the world's most sane and sensible women have fallen under its influence.'

'No,' Cassie repeated. 'I've barely known him a month.'

'I knew with Mason after a week,' Reese said gently.

Cassie snorted—what a debacle *that* had been. 'No,' she said again.

'Okay, then,' Reese said. 'Tell me what you're feeling right now. Tell me what you were feeling just before you cried for twenty minutes. What you've been feeling since Tuck left.'

'Well, it sure as hell isn't *love*,' Cassie said indignantly. 'I feel...'

She petered out. Cassie didn't usually do this sort of thing—talk about her feelings. Her feelings were generally pretty clear-cut. She didn't even know where to start.

'Go on,' Marnie encouraged, moving closer.

'I can't concentrate, and there's this pain in my...gut.

I keep having these memories of our time together that won't stop. I can...*smell* him when he's not around. I can't sleep— and I really, really need to sleep. I eat, but I can't taste the food. I'm not interested in my research. I...I can't even think straight any more.'

Gina, Reese and Marnie looked at each other. Gina winked. Reese grinned. Marnie got the giggles. Then they all laughed.

Cassie glared at them. 'What?' she demanded.

'That *is* love, silly,' Reese said.

Cassie blinked at the utterly ridiculous statement. 'No.' She shook her head.

No one had ever called her silly in her life, and she certainly wasn't going to let Reese get away with it when she'd just made possibly the most absurd statement she'd ever heard.

'I've just rattled off a list that sounds more indicative of a *brain tumour* than anything else and you tell me it's *love? That's* silly.'

She looked at Gina and Marnie, who were nodding their heads in agreement with Reese.

'You have all the symptoms,' Marnie agreed.

'Which you'd know, if you spent more time reading fiction and watching romcoms instead of reading astronomy textbooks and watching science fiction,' Gina added.

They were serious. Deadly serious. And she believed them. If there were three better experts on the subject anywhere in the world she'd be surprised, and they'd never steered her wrong before.

'*This* is love? I thought love was supposed to be *won-*

derful? This doesn't feel wonderful,' she said, looking earnestly at each of her friends, wanting them to tell her they'd made a mistake. 'It feels awful. It...*sucks.*'

Reese laughed. 'That it does.'

'So I'm not going crazy?' she asked, still shaky over her loss of control.

'Nope,' Reese assured her.

Cassie's chest felt tight both in relief and dread. What the hell was she going to do now? Her mother had pretty much spent her life regretting falling in love with her father.

'How do I stop it?' she asked.

Reese shook her head. 'I'm afraid it's terminal. But it *is* manageable. And I promise you can live to a ripe old productive age.'

Marnie hummed 'The Wedding March' and Cassie stared at her. 'I have to *marry* him?' she squeaked. 'That didn't work out so well for my parents. They barely speak to each other.'

'No.' Gina sighed, glaring at Marnie. 'Just...*be* with him. In whatever way that works for you both.'

'Compromise,' Reese agreed. 'You're two smart cookies. You'll work it out. Just listen to your heart.'

'But I...' Cassie's head was spinning. First she'd been sideswiped by her libido and now a foreign emotion was taking over her sensibilities. 'I'm ruled by my head. I'm not ruled by my heart.'

'You are now, hon,' Reese said. 'You are now.'

The next morning Cassie found herself ensconced in Reese's car, heading for New York. She had no idea what she was going to say to Tuck when she got there. She just knew she'd lain awake going over and over it in her head.

The thought that it could really be love she felt for Tuck was still a foreign notion, but her friends were right. Whether she accepted the premise or not, the answer to her conundrum seemed to be Tuck. *Being with Tuck*.

And it was only *logical* to do something about it. To put that part right so her life could fall back into the order she liked and respected.

Reese chatted about her plans for the future with Mason and other inane topics, for which Cassie was thankful, and eventually the miles were gone and Reese had weaved through the New York traffic to deposit Cassie outside her cousin's apartment.

Reese pulled up and dialled Tuck's apartment number on her phone. His gruff. 'What?' confirmed he was inside.

'Good—you're home. I'll be there in a sec,' Reese said pleasantly, and hung up. She turned to face Cassie. 'You're up,' she said, then dragged her in for a big hug. 'Remember,' she said, 'three little words will get you everywhere, okay?'

Cassie nodded, even though she still couldn't quite believe this horrible affliction was *love*. But then they were out of the car and Reese had sweet-talked Cassie past Tuck's doorman, whom she seemed to know quite well, and Cassie was in the lift to the penthouse apartment before she could blink.

Tuck was standing on the other side of it, waiting for the lift doors to open. If Reese thought she could come to his place and blast him over some imagined slight to one of her closest friends—well, she could just turn around and walk away again.

Cassiopeia Barclay had made it more than clear she didn't want him in her life.

The lift dinged, the doors started to slide open and he opened his mouth to let loose his tirade. But it died on his lips as Cassie stood before him.

'Cassie?'

She looked just as he remembered. Terrible fashion sense, carelessly tied back hair, no bra, dark frowny eyebrows, small serious face.

And his heart leapt, hungry at the sight of her.

Cassie didn't move for a while and the lift doors started to slide shut again. Tuck took two strides, slamming his hand up high on either side of the shutting doors, wedging his body in between.

He looked big and blond and scruffy, and his pheromones filled the lift—as lethal to her system as cyanide gas. Her chest filled with the same pain and fullness she hadn't been able to define until Reese had given it a label.

Love.

So it was true. She did love him. Her cells recognised it—they practically buzzed with it. She was suffering a terminal condition and the worst part was the cause was the only cure.

The lift doors succumbed to Tuck's unrelenting hold and jerked open again. 'What do you want?' he asked.

She gulped at the hardness in his voice. 'I'd like to... talk to you.'

'If you're here because you're all horny again, you can forget it. I'm not your own personal plaything.'

Tuck walked away from the lift because he knew he was being a hypocrite. If she so much as looked at him with sex in her eyes he knew she could use him six ways to Sunday and he'd be more than a willing partner.

Just thinking about it gave him a raging hard-on.

Cassie's legs sparked into action as the lift doors started to close again, and she walked into a spacious apartment dominated by the light filtering through massive windows at the far end through which she could see the Manhattan skyline.

'No. I haven't come for...' She faltered. It seemed so bald to speak it aloud. 'It's about something else.'

Tuck headed for his kitchen. He grabbed a heavy glass tumbler from a cupboard and held it beneath the spout of the fridge's ice dispenser. Three cubes made a satisfying clinking noise. The bottle of Scotch which had copped a fair amount of misuse this last week sat on his kitchen bench, almost empty, and it was satisfying to pour the last of its contents over the ice.

He threw back half of it immediately, the burn sucking his breath away. But it was preferable to the burn that had taken up permanent residence in his gut. 'You want a drink?' he asked.

Cassie shook her head. 'No. Thank you.'

They looked at each other across the room. 'Well?' Tuck said eventually as the silence stretched.

'I came to tell you...' She stopped. Those three little words seemed pretty bald, given the way they'd parted, but Reese did know her *love* stuff. 'To tell you that I love you.'

Tuck almost choked on his next, more measured sip of Scotch. They were the words he'd longed to hear a week ago, but the lack of emotion behind them was startling.

'You love me?' he said. 'Just like that?'

'Well, no,' Cassie said, taking a few more steps further into the apartment. 'I'm not good at this. I didn't know that was what it was...this thing. But Reese said—'

Tuck's short, bitter laugh interrupted her. 'Ah, Reese—all loved up and eager to see everyone else loved up as well.'

Cassie frowned. 'No. That's not how it is.'

'Well, how *is* it, then?'

'I can't think or concentrate any more. My research means nothing to me...'

Tuck shrugged. 'So this is about *your* work? Thinking about me interrupts your work? Which brings us back to that libido of yours again. All right, then,' he said, slamming his glass down on the counter, reaching for his belt, undoing it, slipping it through the loops. 'Let's go. Can't have your sex-drive getting in the way of important cosmic research.'

Cassie stepped back, horrified at his suggestion. 'No. I'm trying to tell you...' Tuck pulled his shirt over his head. 'I'm not very good at this stuff.'

His hand was on his zip. The teeth parting seemed loud in the building silence between them. Cassie covered the distance between them, placing her hand on his to halt any further attempts at stripping.

'Please,' she said. 'I'm trying to do this logically, to keep this all straight in my head, and you're not helping.'

Tuck could see desperation shimmering in her blue-grey eyes. It wasn't something he was used to seeing. Could she be telling the truth? *No matter how badly?* Dared he even hope?

'I don't care what's in your head,' he said, poking his index finger at her forehead. 'I don't give a crap about logic.' He needed to know she *felt* something. 'I only care what's in your heart.' He jabbed the same finger into the centre of her chest.

The jab wasn't hard, but Cassie felt it right down to her spine. It stirred unfamiliar feelings. Helplessness. Inadequacy. She wasn't used to feeling like that. Tears welled in her eyes.

'I don't know,' she said, shaking her head as the first tear spilled over. Her nose started to itch and her throat felt as if it was being strangled from the inside. 'I don't *know* what's in it.' A sob came from deep in her chest and more tears fell. 'I've never felt anything inside it before so I don't know how it works.'

Two heaving sobs joined the first, squeezing through her rib-cage, and she tried to breathe and talk but for once in her life she didn't seem able to do two things at once. 'All I know is it's big and deep and messy.' Her face was screwed up, and her words were forced out between sobs. She wasn't sure she was being remotely intelligible. 'And murky. And it threatens to derail everything I know about me and the world around me—'

She stopped then, because she was crying too hard to talk and breathe, but she fought for control because whatever the words that were spewing out of her mouth in an inarticulate mess she needed to say them.

'And it scares the hell out of me because it's something I don't seem to have any control over. And you know how much I need to have control. I feel like I'm going cr...cr...crazy.' She sobbed-hiccoughed. 'And I can't go there again...'

She broke down for a moment, emotion overwhelming her.

'And now I'm cr...cr...crying, and I *never* cry. I've tried to make my head rule my heart...like it always has...but my heart's just not listening any more. It wants what it w-wants, and none of the other stuff m-matters. It's only you that matters.'

Cassie collapsed against his chest, dissolving into more tears. She'd said it. She'd said what was in her heart. She had no idea if it had made any sense—hell, she'd hadn't had a clue her heart had so damn much to say—but it was out now.

Tuck pulled her close as she cried, his heart flying in his chest. 'Shh,' he soothed. 'Shh.'

But it seemed to go on unabated, and he just stood there and held her and let her cry. For a woman who didn't cry she was giving it a good whirl.

But then she had years to make up for.

When it seemed to settle he smiled down at her. Her eyes were red, her neck was all blotchy and she was sniffling. She'd never been more beautiful. He kissed her hard on the mouth.

'Now, *that* was from the heart,' he said as he pulled away.

Cassie wasn't sure if it was a compliment or not, but

he was grinning down at her, and when he said, 'I love you too,' she finally relaxed.

'You're not going crazy,' he said, looking down into her tearstained face, because he understood how much that prospect terrified her. 'You're just getting in touch with your emotional side.'

'I don't like my emotional side,' she said, and sniffed.

Tuck chuckled. 'That's okay, because I love it.' He kissed her again. 'We're getting married,' he said. 'Soon.'

Cassie blinked. *That* she hadn't expected. 'Why?'

'Because that's the next *logical* move when you're in love,' he said, dropping a kiss on her nose.

'Isn't that a little rushed, though?'

'Sure—for some. But I reckon we both know what we want, and after years of not knowing, I don't want to waste any more time.'

'But there's so much we need to talk about,' she said. 'What about Antarctica? What about that family you want?'

'Cassiopeia, I'm not going to stop you from going to Antarctica or pursuing any part of your career.'

Cassie's heart leapt at his words. 'But...you seemed hesitant about it last time...at the apartment...the night you left.'

'Of course.' He smiled, his hands cradling her cheeks. 'Six months is a long time. I'm going to miss you like crazy. But I'll survive.' He kissed her long and slow to punctuate his commitment.

When he was finished he dropped his hands.

'As for a family—I don't mean we have to have one straight away. We're young. We've got time. And it doesn't have to be a traditional family. We can adopt. We can foster a kid from the system. We can get a surrogate. And you don't have to give up work. You have me, and I'm going to make a freaking great dad. My job is portable and we have the means.'

Cassie's head spun. 'You have this all worked out, don't you?'

Tuck nodded. 'I do. All you have to say is *I do* too and we'll work it out. When it makes sense to be together, why delay?'

Cassie couldn't fault his logic. And logic she understood. 'I do,' she said.

Tuck grinned and swept her in his arms, crushing a kiss against her mouth that had her clinging and moaning for more as her senses filled with his wild Tuck pheromones.

'Damn straight you do,' Tuck muttered against her mouth, before swinging her up into his arms and introducing her to his bedroom.

* * * * *

Look for Gina's story in
MAID OF DISHONOR
Coming soon